# The explosion of the gunshot rocked Finn…

Even though he'd been expecting it, it was almost worse than the first one.

He heard Jordyn yelp and his heart dropped.

"I'm fine!" she called ahead. She muttered something he didn't hear. "Hurry. I want to get out of here."

Getting out of here was the best idea they'd had all day. There had been a note with the body her K-9 found, though they hadn't been able to read it before the killer took aim. They were the targets, since whoever was shooting at them could clearly see who they were. He ducked and ran, with Jordyn close behind him. Even the dog, Cipher, seemed to get low as they moved quickly across the boulder field. They just had to make it to the shelter of the trees…

But even if they did, after being attacked and left for dead, after someone almost ran Jordyn off the road, he didn't think this was the end of it.

The killer wanted them dead.

**Sarah Varland** lives in Alaska with her husband, John, their two boys and their dogs. Her passion for books comes from her mom; her love for suspense comes from her dad, who has spent a career in law enforcement. When she's not writing, she's often found dog mushing, hiking, reading, kayaking, drinking coffee or enjoying other Alaskan adventures with her family.

### Books by Sarah Varland

### Love Inspired Suspense

Visit the Author Profile page at LoveInspired.com.

# HUNTING
# A KILLER

## SARAH VARLAND

**LOVE INSPIRED SUSPENSE**
INSPIRATIONAL ROMANCE

**MIX**
Paper | Supporting responsible forestry
FSC
www.fsc.org
**FSC® C021394**

## LOVE INSPIRED® SUSPENSE
### INSPIRATIONAL ROMANCE

Recycling programs for this product may not exist in your area.

ISBN-13: 978-1-335-95751-1

Hunting a Killer

Copyright © 2026 by Sarah Varland

Love Inspired
22 Adelaide St. West, 41st Floor
Toronto, Ontario M5H 4E3, Canada
www.LoveInspired.com

HarperCollins Publishers
Macken House, 39/40 Mayor Street Upper,
Dublin 1, D01 C9W8, Ireland
www.HarperCollins.com

**Printed in Lithuania**

For God so loved the world, that he gave his only begotten Son, that whosoever believeth in him should not perish, but have everlasting life.
—*John* 3:16

To my family.

# ONE

If he hurried, he just might get there in time, Finn Mc-Daniel told himself as he pressed down on the accelerator, navigating the winding mountain road. The window was open, and the Alaskan summer air was cool today, the sky overcast, and it was one of those days where Finn didn't think he'd miss it at all when he finally got out.

Seven years in the Bureau, eight years since his sister had disappeared, nine years since the last time he could remember really loving the place where he lived. Alaska's wildness, its untamed spirit and beauty juxtaposed with ever-present danger had seemed a lot more appealing to him before Tori's death. Since then…really, he just wanted to be somewhere safer. More controlled. Less wild.

His bosses had promised he was almost free. One more case, they'd said. Then word had come into the Anchorage field office where he worked that the small town of Eagle Bend—his hometown—was dealing with a serial killer. He'd packed his bags and headed to the location on the Kenai Peninsula where the killer was operating, cautiously optimistic that it might wrap up quickly and he could be on his way to a new posting in another state. Finally.

If only they had realized how much this case had in common with the one that still haunted his dreams, maybe Finn wouldn't have been the one assigned to it.

Forcing his mind onto the present and out of the past—or at least trying to—he drove to a trailhead he remembered liking as a kid. This was the same location that law enforcement had relentlessly searched for his sister's body. And never found it.

So far, everybody this serial killer had killed had been found here. At first it seemed similar to a case Finn remembered hearing about a few years ago in another Alaskan town, where women who hiked in a certain wilderness area were being stalked and murdered. Yet as more women kept disappearing, it became obvious that wasn't what was happening here. The FBI still didn't know what was motivating this killer's selection of women, or exactly how he or she was luring them away from their safe lives and killing them, but they were confident of one thing: the victims weren't always killed here, but the bodies always ended up here.

He parked in a rush and hopped out of his vehicle, then started the hike faster than he usually did, enjoying the feeling of his legs burning as he pushed his pace and moved from the well-traveled main trail onto a side trail. He was choosing by instinct now; his information hadn't been specific enough to predict exactly where in the vast backcountry the next victim might be. Nor did he have any guarantee that the next victim would still be alive when he got there. What he did have, finally, was a lead on timing. The pattern he had just figured out regarding how much time typically passed between murders was dependent on several factors, but in this instance in particular, he felt confident the next murder was going to occur today. And very soon. He had to hurry.

He had no idea who the victim would be, since no women

had been reported missing. He didn't know a motive. But he *did* know that according to the MO details he'd only just pieced together, by noticing a pattern in the women who had died so far, someone would be killed here today.

Desperation pushed him forward. He'd hardly let himself consider on the drive over that it was possible he might be able to stop a murder, but now he found himself hoping. Wishing.

He rounded a corner, moved quietly through the trees, catching a glimpse of movement in a clearing and moving in that direction. A figure. Maybe two.

All of his adult life, Finn's main goal as an FBI agent had been to stop crimes before they happened, to dismantle plans, untangle threads and prevent tragedy from wrecking someone else's life the way it had wrecked his and his family's.

And he'd failed this time, he saw just as he neared the edge of the trees.

He saw the woman—he couldn't tell much about her from this distance besides that she was of a medium build and her hair was brown. Gunfire exploded through the air, making his ears ring, and the way she crumpled instantly left no doubt that she was dead, and he knew without having seen it exactly how she would have been shot. It would be one to the forehead, execution style, just like all the others.

Even knowing it was too late to help her, it hurt to stand still. To just watch as the body lay there. But he had to do this right. Backup should be arriving any second. When he'd pieced together the details of the case and realized today could be the day that they caught whoever was behind these murders, he'd left a message through a coworker at the FBI and had followed up since to make sure agents were on their way.

Seconds ticked into minutes. The figure—he couldn't tell anything about their identity under the dark, oversize clothes and a black hood—stood still.

It was a horrible silence, stretched and long.

Backup should be here. Why weren't they here? He didn't know why the killer was hanging around so long, or if they were likely to continue to do so. This was not a killer who did anything particularly sick with the bodies of his or her victims—besides actually killing them. The kills were clean. According to the medical examiner he worked with, the victims never suffered from pain from the fatal wound for long…death was fairly instantaneous. Was the killer just waiting to make sure the woman was dead?

The killer started to move, and he felt himself flinch. He couldn't lose them. This was the closest anyone had gotten to the perp.

And he wasn't going to let them get away. He stepped forward, hearing the slight noise his feet made as he shifted his weight and moved through the low-lying vegetation. He crept closer and closer. Twenty feet. Fifteen feet. Ten feet. Five. Three.

He didn't want to shoot. But he pulled his gun out anyway, not willing to be unprepared. He needed to bring this criminal in alive so they could truly face justice for what they'd done. He also wouldn't announce himself too early and give the killer a chance to flee.

The person standing over the body turned. Finn's eyes widened as he recognized the killer. Not who he'd anticipated. Their eyes locked.

"It's you," he said, understanding and horror dawning at the same time, even as he raised his weapon, realizing it might be his only choice.

"Yes, it's me." The voice was evil. Jarringly so.

The killer's weapon was up and firing again before Finn knew what was happening, and he jumped to dodge the shot, landing in a way that had him off balance. Too close to the killer. A flash of movement caught his eye as the killer flung an arm forward.

Finn felt the impact of something heavy against his head, felt the immediate explosion of pain as his skull took the hit. It felt like the sound of something shattering reverberated through his head in echoes of pain and then...

Nothing. Everything was darkness.

With every step that Jordyn Williams took, she knew she was walking straight toward death. Not hers, someone else's, but the weighty feeling on her shoulders never quite left her alone, no matter how many bodies she and her human-remains detection dog, Cipher, found. As she made her way through the thick forest, past old-growth spruce and low brambles, she prayed she would find the body soon.

Finding the young woman alive would be so much better, but Jordyn had given up on that more than twenty-four hours ago. A serial killer on Alaska's Kenai Peninsula wasn't letting any of them hope much these days. The murders were far enough apart, anywhere from four weeks to four months, that people started to relax.

Then someone else would disappear, setting everyone on edge again.

Some of the victims were presumed victims, missing women whose bodies were as yet undiscovered.

Most, Jordyn and Cipher had found. She'd never get used to it.

Following her mostly white husky farther into the backcountry, Jordyn pressed on as the light from the sun dimmed and she hiked farther into the spruce forest. There were many trails in this part of the Kenai woods—some single track trails, some hiking trails, mostly game trails—but they'd left the established trail several miles back. There was more than enough daylight this time of year, and she'd have enough usable light to continue the search well past ten o'clock. The only question was, could she and Cipher make it that long? She had snacks for both of them in the pack on her back, plenty of water, but this was a draining endeavor both for the human handler and the search dog, and Jordyn didn't want to push either of them too far.

Taking a deep breath, Jordyn looked around her, keeping a sense of what was going on in her peripheral vision. The woods were quiet and still today. The soft dirt under her feet gave beneath her weight, like the moss below was a cushion. It smelled spicy and woodsy, like spruce needles and fresh air, and it was hard for Jordyn to reconcile the fact that the woods were always where she felt the most relaxed, where she felt a sense of peace, despite that someone had taken to shattering that sense of peace and using the wilderness to hide bodies.

The MO of this particular serial killer was nothing elaborate. One single gunshot wound to center mass. The victim would be in her twenties. Buried or left for dead—they'd found several women in both states—in the wilderness but according to no particular pattern they'd been able to find as far as proximity to water, landmarks or anything else. Jordyn hadn't given up hoping that there was some pattern, something they could use, but if there was, they hadn't found it yet. They needed a break. Something, anything, to give them more of a sense of who the suspect could be. As a search and rescue worker, Jordyn wasn't always given details about cases or their progress or resolution, but she wanted to know updates on this one if at all possible. The lack of resolution when someone lost a loved one kept her awake at night.

Had for five years, since her normally calm life had been interrupted by the disappearance of her best friend, Tori McDaniel. She'd been in college at the time, in Washington. But when Jordyn heard that Tori had disappeared, she'd flown home and practically lived at the local SAR command center waiting for updates.

There had been few.

The search had eventually been called off, the case deemed cold. It was that feeling, the hopelessness, the lack of closure, that had made Jordyn stop pursuing her degree in psychology and return home to train search dogs instead.

Pushing her past from the front of her mind, though cases like this one made it particularly difficult with all the similarities, Jordyn continued ahead. Cipher had picked up her pace, but that didn't necessarily mean anything. Sometimes she just moved faster than others. Jordyn could hope, though. And right now she was hoping it meant Cipher had caught a scent on the air currents, something that would lead them to where this most recent body was stashed.

Cipher lifted her nose, and Jordyn felt her own breath catch. The K-9 had something. She was almost positive. The dog sped up and Jordyn followed, jogging easily over roots, thankful for how she'd acclimated to the backcountry. Before Tori had disappeared, Jordyn never would have considered herself comfortable in the wilderness. She enjoyed the outdoors, liked hiking, but she never quite felt at home outside like some people did. Her confidence being alone in the woods had been built over time.

Still, it didn't mean she was immune to having shivers run down her spine, as they were now. This often happened when Cipher was close to alerting, and Jordyn could tell.

Because underneath her excitement and the feeling that they were going to bring a case one step closer to being solved was the underlying knowledge that they were coming closer to a body.

The realization never got any easier. It hit just as hard every single time.

Darting right, Cipher sprinted up ahead even faster now and Jordyn hurried to follow. Then the dog stopped, laid down and let out a long, mournful howl.

She'd found the victim.

It was difficult to see through the trees, but it looked to Jordyn like there was a small clearing in the woods ahead. She could see Cipher fairly well, but she was lying down beside the body she'd found. All Jordyn could tell was that it was the right size to be a person, though it might be slightly taller than the barely-over-five-feet woman she'd been searching for.

Taking a deep breath of air, she found herself noting the lack of any smell of decomposition. At least this woman's family hadn't had days of wondering, of false hopes being raised then shattered in pieces. They'd only reported the woman, Nicole Collins, missing a few hours ago, and Jordyn had immediately started searching. Those were her only consolations as Jordyn braced herself, shoulders back, and started forward. She'd need to reward Cipher for her find, call in the woman's body...

Except... It wasn't a woman.

Jordyn blinked. On the ground beside Cipher was an adult male, dressed in hiking gear as though he'd been doing something similar to what Jordyn was—intentionally trekking through the woods. He was on his back, his head apparently having sustained some kind of trauma, judging by the contusions and blood on the side.

It seemed for a minute like the wilderness held its breath while Jordyn tried to process. This wasn't the body she'd been expecting. Still, she'd have to call it in. Reaching for her radio, she knelt beside the man, ready to breathe a short prayer like she did for the loved ones of every single person she and Cipher found. She closed her eyes.

She heard the slight shift a second before her mind had a chance to react, and then there was something—someone?—gripping her arm.

In her effort to jerk away from whatever had grabbed her—surely not the body—Jordyn threw herself backward and hit the ground hard on her backside. Cipher had stood also and was by Jordyn's side, her head down, alert.

The body on the ground was moving.

And then his eyes opened. He reached out again, deliberately, for Jordyn's arm, which she pulled away.

"Help me. You have to help me," he said, then his eyelids fluttered, and he fell to the ground again.

Not a body. Bodies didn't look at you with fear in their brown eyes and beg you for help. If she'd thought her mind was racing before, it was going double, no triple time now.

She had to call this in. This man was hurt and needed help.

"Please." He was talking again, but this time almost as if in his sleep. He flailed on the ground, and Jordyn reached out a hand to try to settle him, resting it on his shoulder. "Shhh, it's okay." It was not an intentional lie, but she was aware as she said it that she had no idea if it was okay or not. She only knew it couldn't be good for his head injury for him to keep hitting his head on the ground like that. Her EMT training made her extra conscientious of the danger of head injuries, especially repeated ones.

"Don't let them shoot me, don't let them…"

"It's okay. I'm going to call the police."

"No!" He sat up again, wobbling a little from how fast he'd moved. He groaned, put his hand to his head. "No police. Please." Reaching up a hand, he rubbed his forehead and blinked. Jordyn thought maybe he was regaining full consciousness, and she felt herself tense. There was nothing to say this man wasn't the serial killer who'd been terrorizing the area, though he certainly didn't fit her mental picture of a serial killer. He was personable looking. Short blond hair, clearly fit, his brown eyes warm, though full of terror. He looked like a man comfortable in the outdoors, but also like he could star in a made-for-TV movie where he helped the heroine learn to thrive on her recently inherited horse ranch in the country. But looks could be deceiving, and Jordyn didn't like taking risks.

It was times like this that she wished she wasn't so opposed to guns. She wasn't necessarily opposed to them on the whole, but she wasn't very comfortable using or carrying one, which made her feel somewhat unusual in a state where it was the standard for people to hike with a weapon. She felt at a huge disadvantage with only a container of bear spray with which to defend herself.

"I have to call this in," she said.

"You can't. I'll be killed… There was a gun…and she's dead already…"

"Who's dead?" The missing woman?

His eyebrows knit together in a frown. "I don't know."

Hand halfway to her phone, Jordyn paused. "You don't know what?"

"I don't know who killed her."

"I probably should call EMS for that head wound, and I definitely have to call the police if you saw someone get killed."

"No. I can't trust everyone there. They'll kill me if you call it in."

"Who?"

Another beat of silence. A deeper frown on his face. "I don't know."

She'd met all kinds of people in her time in SAR. It wasn't unusual for people to be at their worst when she came into contact with them, out of sorts, dehydrated, suffering from exposure. This man…concussion? Or was he impaired somehow?

She looked at his eyes again. They were familiar, even though she didn't believe they'd ever met. Clear, not bloodshot. His pleading seemed genuine. The fear in his eyes couldn't be manufactured.

She'd ask his name and what he was doing out here, then go from there.

Jordyn leaned toward him just in time to see him fall back onto the ground. She winced as his head hit the dirt. Then, hesitating only for a second, she reached for the wallet that had worked its way out of his pocket in the struggle and was now lying beside him on the ground.

The first letters that caught her attention were FBI. It was common knowledge that the FBI had been called in to assist the local police department with finding the serial killer. This man must be one of them.

The second thing she noticed was his name. Finn McDaniel.

Her missing friend Tori's brother.

# TWO

Dragging a full-grown man out of the woods on her own strength had not been part of the plan for today, but as Jordyn stared down at Finn, she was hoping she had enough in her backpack to make it work. Fashioning some kind of sling, a drag…she could probably make it happen…

He hadn't recognized her. Because of his head injury or how long it had been since they'd last seen each other? Probably the latter, since Jordyn hadn't recognized him either. They'd stayed out of each other's way during the search for Tori, since Jordyn had been fascinated by the search dogs and their handlers and how the K-9s were able to catch a scent and work with it, and Finn had put a little more of his faith into the law enforcement side. She remembered that even then he'd been planning on a career in law enforcement, but she seemed to recall Tori saying that her brother had wanted to work at the town police department. Tori had been happy he would still be close, besides a short stint down in Sitka at the law enforcement academy. It must have been after Tori's disappearance that Finn decided to join the FBI. Was he working up here regularly? Or had he been flown up just for this case?

Jordyn felt a sudden zap of connection as she studied him. He was perhaps the only person who would feel the same way she did about working this serial killer case. While it wasn't exactly like Tori's, trying to find the bodies of missing women in the Alaskan wilderness did hit close to home for her.

It was that lack of closure, that resounding, reverberating grief in her own life, that made her show up for this job day after day. She didn't want anyone else to have to experience that. Ever.

Slowly, Finn sat up, blinking.

"I hate to ask this, but do you think you can try to walk? It would be easier to get us both out of here if you could." She had her doubts that this was a good idea—he probably needed a medevac—but if Finn thought he couldn't trust the police, she'd give him the benefit of the doubt and wouldn't call this in just yet.

He stood slowly, as though trying to get his bearings, and managed to move forward. He was clearly disoriented, but she put his arm around her shoulder and used her body to brace his. He was stronger than she'd expected after whatever ordeal he had been through. Somehow, she managed to steer both of them back to her car, and mercifully no one was in the parking lot to see them. If Finn was serious about someone being after him and this wasn't some kind of fever dream on his part, Jordyn didn't want to take chances with him being observed, both for his safety and for her own. She loaded him into the passenger seat, noting that he seemed to be fading out of consciousness again. Shutting the door, she hurried around the car and slid into the passenger seat.

"Who are you?" he looked over at her and asked.

"Jordyn Williams. Your sister's friend?"

His eyes clouded over. "And who…who am I?"

Her eyebrows rose. Amnesia wasn't uncommon after

head trauma, but long-term amnesia was a little different than the short-term. "You're Finn McDaniel. Sound familiar?"

"Finn..." He trailed off.

Who had done this to him? The blood on his head was dry and caking, but it hurt her to look at. How he'd managed to walk out of the woods, she didn't know, though she was thankful that he'd stayed conscious long enough to do so.

"I really wish you'd let me call for help," she said barely above a whisper as she put the car in gear. He looked like he was sleeping now. Something about his vulnerability tugged at her heartstrings a bit. This wasn't at all like the Finn that she remembered. He'd been arrogant and overconfident. This man appeared broken. And yet he must still have a flicker of that fighting spirit or he'd likely be in worse shape right now.

"No police. No FBI," came his urgent voice.

She glanced over at him. He hadn't mentioned the FBI earlier.

"Why?" Jordyn asked, taking a chance that he would answer.

"Someone...someone told them..." He trailed off again. There were too many possible answers for what could fit in the gaps. Jordyn didn't want to speculate. Still, he seemed convinced, and after what had happened to his sister, Jordyn wasn't willing to take any chances with his life.

But was that what she was doing by not calling for an ambulance?

She looked over at him again.

"Please," he whispered before he went still again.

One night. She'd give him one night, or at least most of it. His breathing was steady. She'd check over him better when they got to her house. Her EMT training was enough to give him that. If he showed any signs of a brain bleed, she'd haul him into Soldotna, the nearest town of any size, to the emergency room.

She drove back to her place and parked in her driveway, thankful she had no close neighbors to watch her attempts to get him inside.

Getting him out of the car was more difficult than getting him in had been, but she managed, Cipher beside them the entire time as though she was supervising. The dog didn't seem alarmed by Finn's presence, which was a good sign. Jordyn would trust her dog's opinion of a person's character any day.

She settled him down onto the couch in the small apartment that adjoined her house. It was lower than the bed and easier to maneuver him onto. There was a solid lock between her side of the house and this apartment, which she sometimes used to generate rental income—if she'd misjudged and Finn was a danger to her at all, she should be safe.

It was difficult to do any kind of neuro exam with him drifting in and out of consciousness, but she sat by him for a little while, and when he would have moments of wakefulness she did her best to see if he was capable of passing the tests that would indicate the injury likely hadn't had serious consequences. Eventually satisfied that it was likely a concussion and not something more serious, she finally sat back against a chair beside the couch, watching him sleep, trying to decide if she should go back to her side of the house.

Leaving him felt strange, though, so she moved to the kitchen, pulled out a mug and her French press, and set about making herself a cup of coffee.

Every noise caught her attention, every creak of the

house seemed malevolent. Her mind searched for answers, wanted to believe somehow that what had happened to Finn was an accident, but the proof was in front of her eyes, sleeping fitfully on the sofa, occasionally muttering, "They killed her... They killed her..."

It was enough to send chills down her spine. With Cipher on the floor, stretched out, Jordyn kept watch, listened for any sounds that were out of the ordinary.

Because while he was unconscious and clearly not entirely in his right mind, everything he'd said made sense. This case felt different than any other she'd helped SAR with. For one, the person committing the murders knew how to avoid detection. Her boss had lost weight from the stress of it. She and Finn McDaniel may have had a long list of things they didn't see eye to eye on, but ultimately, she trusted him. Would trust him with her life if necessary.

And right now, he had to trust her with his. Because something was happening, more than she knew about yet. And it looked like Jordyn had just put herself in the crossfire.

Everything around Finn was blackness, and it was suffocating him. Or maybe the killer was suffocating him. She was dead...the victim...and now he was next...

He rolled over, groaned at the pain that came with the movement, and then realized his eyes were shut. Was he dreaming? Had it all been a dream?

He opened his eyes, or at least he thought he had, but it was just as dark. He felt for his sidearm at his waist. Gone.

Immediately he sat up, the fear from his dreams having followed him into real life, and as he did so a fresh wave of pain and dizziness exploded in his head. He winced against it, trying to make sense of what had happened, why he hurt so badly. It hadn't been a dream, he'd seen the killer, and then…and then…

Blackness. Darkness.

Then someone clicked a lamp on. "Shh. Hey. Don't hurt yourself, okay?"

A female voice. Not one he recognized, though there was something familiar about it. He looked over at her.

She didn't look like a threat, but he knew better than to judge based on appearances. Her hair was the color of birch leaves in late fall, a dark red that seemed to glow in the light of the lamp she'd turned on. She wore an oversize white sweater, hair piled on her head in some cozy kind of style.

"Who are you?" he asked, still wincing against the throbbing of his head. Had she put him in this state? She looked tall. But he was tall himself at a couple inches over six feet—surely she wouldn't have been able to get the jump on him?

"I'm Jordyn Williams."

"Jordyn… Tori's friend, right?" Her facial muscles relaxed, or at least he thought they did. "What is it?"

"It's just…you know who I am. And who Tori is—that's a good sign."

The pain in his head intensified. He squeezed his eyes shut. Winced. "Why wouldn't I know who she is? Was?"

"You didn't know much yesterday. You asked me what my name was and what your name was. I told you I was Tori's friend Jordyn and that you were—"

"Finn McDaniel."

"Exactly."

"Someone must have attacked me. Or something happened. My head hurts." It was an understatement, but it was all he could manage as he struggled to catch up. "How did I… What happened?"

"I'm not entirely sure. My dog, Cipher, found you. It's a good thing she did." She nodded to a good-size husky who was eyeing him from a few feet away with a measure of suspicion in her eyes. Well, the husky could get in line. He felt suspicious and uncomfortable with this whole situation too. He wasn't suspicious of Jordyn, necessarily. She and Tori had been best friends, and he'd watched her grow up. But the entire situation was confusing, and that made him feel…

Well, anxious. Not an emotion he was particularly comfortable with. "Walk me through it. Where were we?"

"You don't remember any of that?" She tilted her head to the side a little. He felt a bit like a science experiment, like she was observing him and making notes about how he was doing.

"No… I just remember…"

"Shh." She put a finger to her lips, silencing him.

Finn stopped talking. Listened.

He heard nothing. He looked around instead, decided that if one sense was failing him, he should see what the other could pick up on. Cipher, Jordyn's dog, wasn't in the room anymore.

Finn struggled to sit up, to get to a position where he could see better. There the dog was, near the front of the house…cabin…whatever this place was. Her ears were up and her eyes were serious, fixed on something in front of them.

She let out a low growl, the sound starting deep in her chest then echoing, growing louder as it came out of her mouth. The noise was spine-chilling, a reminder of a husky's connection to their distant wild ancestors.

What did she hear?

Cipher flinched, moved toward the door. The growling intensified.

Seconds later, Finn heard a faint noise. Quiet, but like the click of metal against metal. Someone rattling the door knob? "Is that…" He started to ask Jordyn, who was still sitting in the chair across from him, though he noticed she'd moved to the edge of it, her muscles tensed, like she was about to stand.

"Front door," she said in a voice barely louder than a whisper.

Finn felt trapped in his own body. If he tried to move, would he pass out again? His head throbbed, but that wasn't going to stop him. What he didn't want was to be a liability to Jordyn, end up getting her killed. He couldn't remember much…but he knew he'd seen the murderer. Who was it? He had to remember. What he'd seen put him in immense danger—and now Jordyn was in danger too. Frustration simmered as he stood slowly, reaching out to steady his hand on the sofa.

"Where's my gun?" he asked.

Her eyebrows shot up, the expression on her face speaking plainly. Yes, he had a head injury. Was him having a weapon a good idea, by the book? No. But—call him crazy—he didn't like the idea of facing a potential serial killer without one.

"It's put away. You can have it back when you need it and when I'm sure you're stable."

That was fair. He couldn't really argue with that.

"But…" He trailed off anyway, still uncomfortable with the vulnerable position he'd put them both in by bringing danger to her door.

She reached into the drawer of the small table next to

her and stood, pulling out a small revolver as she did so. "I have one. And I know how to use it if I have to."

Great.

He'd have to trust her to protect both of them, even though he probably had the better training. It wasn't like he had a choice.

The rattling of the doorknob grew longer. He heard the wood of the door groan as someone slammed against it.

Cipher barked. A deep warning bark.

The noise stopped. The room went silent.

Finn held his breath. Had they left? Or were they just going to find another way to get in?

# THREE

The shattering of glass broke the silence as shards rained down somewhere in the house. Jordyn didn't know where it was but thought it was near the front of her place, through the door that connected the apartment to the rest of her house.

"Stay here," Jordyn said to Finn then, realizing he wasn't likely to listen to her, she hurried through the door and slammed it shut, locking it from the other side once she and Cipher were through.

She didn't like the idea of facing whoever had broken in alone, but a man with a major concussion wasn't going to be able to provide much help anyway. And besides, if whoever had broken in was after him, maybe they'd leave when they looked around and couldn't find him.

A little farfetched, but she could hope.

Jordyn reached the small kitchen, which adjoined a cozy living room, and struggled to make sense of what she saw. Broken glass. A figure moving toward her. Large.

Cipher immediately put herself between Jordyn and the intruder, which Jordyn both hated and appreciated. The dog was trained for search and rescue, but practically speaking, she was often the only protection Jordyn had. This was far from the first time Cipher had stood between her and danger, whether it be of the human or bear variety.

Jordyn held the gun up, aimed at the intruder and tried to calm her shaking hands. She'd been telling Finn the truth earlier when she told him she knew how to use it, but just because she had the knowledge didn't mean she was comfortable with it. Guns for her were somewhere down past last resort.

The intruder charged her, knocked her back, and Jordyn barely stopped herself from falling over. Blindly, Jordyn tried to fight back, but she was clearly losing. Hand-to-hand combat wasn't something she knew anything about. Something heavy connected with her shoulder, and she cried out in pain.

Something clattered. A chair? She heard Cipher growling. Snarling.

This time the yell wasn't Jordyn's but the intruder's. Had Cipher bitten the intruder?

Jordyn sat up, ignoring the throb of pain in her shoulder, and watched as the intruder—dressed entirely in black, tall but not too tall—moved toward Cipher.

"No!" She yelled.

She couldn't fire the gun; they were all too close in proximity, and Cipher was moving too unpredictably. She couldn't risk hitting the dog.

Instead, Jordyn picked up a pillow that had fallen off the couch, stood up and rushed at the intruder, wielding the pillow like some kind of weapon, slinging it side to side. In the chaos, Cipher must have attacked the intruder again, because Jordyn heard another yell and then the intruder was running. Back through the busted window. Outside into the predawn light.

Everything was still. But not calm. Her heart was racing in her chest, her hands were shaking even more now as Jordyn surveyed the wreck left behind. The window was destroyed. She had plywood in the garage they could repair it with, but it was still a problem. Dining room chairs all over the floor. No blood, she noticed, somehow looking for that detail, probably because it was something she was used to searching for when she was working SAR. If Cipher had bitten the intruder as Jordyn suspected she had, the blood hadn't leaked onto the floor. Injuries would be more annoying than debilitating, which explained how the attacker been able to run from the room.

"You okay?" She reached over toward Cipher, checked on the dog but found no signs of injuries. Satisfied that Cipher was okay, she sat for a minute. Breathing. Bracing herself. Finn. She had to check on Finn.

Jordyn called for Cipher to follow her, and went back through the adjoining door. She locked it behind her on the apartment side since the window was broken and they'd have no auditory warning if the intruder came through it again.

Finn. Finn looked awful, his face even paler. He was standing just on the other side of the door, looking as angry as she'd ever seen him.

"You should lie back down," she said, finding the words a strange way to break the silence in the aftermath of so much danger and chaos, but not knowing what else to say. Concussion protocol certainly didn't call for the injured person to get involved in hand-to-hand combat like that.

"I can't believe you locked me in here." He groaned as he held a hand up to his head but didn't move from where he was sitting on the floor.

"You're in no shape to fight like this." He opened his mouth to argue, but she cut him off. "Seriously, you have to lie back down." Her EMT training seemed to have over-ridden the trauma of the last few minutes, as Jordyn focused her energy on getting him back into a position where he wouldn't do anymore damage to himself. She moved to where he was on the floor and offered her hand to help him up, which he took without arguing. Probably an indication of how badly he was hurting right now.

"I have to get out of here," Finn mumbled even as he lay back down on the pillows.

"You can't leave with this kind of head injury unless you're going straight to the hospital."

"No. No one can know I'm alive…" He trailed off. "Except someone does know now. And you're in danger because of it."

"You don't know that. Whoever that was could have been after me. Or something here at my house. We may have just been in their way."

Except who would want to break into her house? The obvious answer for someone working on a serial killer case was the killer, of course, but she hadn't done anything particularly helpful so far in this case. Yes, she and Cipher had found several bodies, so technically they had contributed to the investigation that way, but it wasn't as though she had helped the police department come any closer to solving the case, and she didn't have anything in the house that could be considered evidence that might incriminate someone. Unless her search logs, which she kept a copy of at home, could be considered integral to the case.

"What would they have been after?" Finn asked the question aloud, seeming to echo her own thoughts. She looked over at him and shook her head, feeling how serious her face must look. That was how she felt. Somber. Aware of the fact that someone was…

What? After her? That seemed strong. Someone… someone had tried to break into her house. And her gut told her it wasn't a random incident or attempted robbery. But maybe she should keep it simple and stick to the facts of what had happened. No reason to jump to conclusions.

The memory of Cipher's low, rattling growl made her shudder. Whoever had been there had not been a friend, she felt sure enough about that.

"This has never happened to me before," Jordyn admitted. "I mean, I've worked a lot of cases, even some where a bad actor was suspected, but no one has ever come to my house. I wonder if they think I saw something yesterday. Maybe they were watching me work the scene? Saw me find you… I made sure I wasn't followed on the way home, to the best of my ability, after you told me someone was after you. But when I first found you, I was working it like a regular scene. Most of my attention was on Cipher, not my surroundings."

Jordyn envisioned the scene yesterday, her kneeling beside Finn's still form. Then she imagined someone at the edge of the woods. Watching. Silent.

She shivered. Swallowed hard.

"It's my fault," he mumbled. "What if whoever is after me knows that I'm here?"

"There's no way. I watched to make sure no one was following me." It had seemed like slight overkill to her at the time, but since she didn't really know why someone would have attacked Finn, unless it was the killer, she'd decided it was better to be safe than sorry.

"That said, I'm not sure you can be sure."

She turned to argue with him, even had her mouth open to do so, but closed it at the last minute. Instead of the cocky expression she'd been anticipating, he looked humble and a little uncertain. She swallowed back the words. "Maybe you're right."

"I didn't mean…"

"I know."

Was this really the same man she'd argued with the last time she'd seen him? They'd both been on edge, hanging out around anyone involved in his sister's case, hoping for word, or better yet, hoping that Tori herself would materialize unharmed and safe.

They hadn't gotten that, though, and they'd been strongly opinionated about finding answers in different ways. Jordyn kept encouraging search and rescue workers to utilize the dogs more. Search dogs were nothing new to Alaska, even five years ago, but the traditional-leaning police chief at the time hadn't wanted to trust dogs over search tactics he was more familiar with. Jordyn and Finn had disagreed on that point, and it hadn't been too polite. She knew she'd called him arrogant and couldn't remember exactly what else she'd said to him, though it probably hadn't been pleasant. She'd been hurting over the loss of her friend, lashing out, and they hadn't spoken since.

"About before. Years ago…"

"Probably about time we let that go, don't you think?" His voice was understanding, kind.

Jordyn nodded slowly as the words soaked into her psyche. They couldn't let it go, not in the sense that they could pretend Tori's disappearance and the turmoil that followed, waiting months and then years for answers, hadn't affected them. Look at them, choosing their entire future career paths based on that experience. But maybe it was better that they do their best to let the past stay there.

The only problem was that, in Jordyn's experience, the past rarely stayed where it belonged.

"Speaking of the past…" she started and watched his face tense. "Not that far past. Just yesterday…we need to talk about yesterday."

His expression seemed to relax; the color of his eyes even lightened slightly. She wasn't sure she'd ever seen someone's eye color be tied to their mood, but Finn's somehow seemed to be. She blinked a couple of times, trying to determine their exact color, whether they were more brown than green, when she realized she was staring. He really was handsome. He'd been cute as a teenager, and she hadn't been immune. But grown up, he was gorgeous.

"Um…" She cleared her throat and looked away. "You seem to have experienced some kind of memory loss."

"Which I still have today because I have no idea how I ended up like this." His voice was wry, and she admired him for trying to find some lightness in a heavy situation.

"Sure, but yesterday you didn't know who I was, and worse, you had no idea who you were or of your connection with the FBI. You said some things warning me not to trust the police or the FBI, but your recall seemed to be affected by whatever happened before I found you. Do you remember being attacked? I wanted to bring you to the hospital…" She trailed off, waiting to see if he remembered.

"But?" he asked.

"But you insisted that it wasn't safe. That someone was after you and I could trust no one. So I brought you here. I'm EMT certified, and it's not enough. I don't have enough here to thoroughly treat a head injury, but I do have enough to recognize the serious warning signs that would have required an immediate hospital visit despite the risks."

"Since the risk is someone murdering me, I'm not sure I agree there would have been a point at which forcing me to go to the hospital was the right call, but go on."

"Anyway, this morning—if we can call it morning this early—you know who you are. You know who I am. Your condition is much improved."

"But I still don't know how I got like this."

"Short-term amnesia isn't uncommon for a head injury like yours." She was glad he remembered the major things and wasn't exhibiting signs of long-term memory loss, yet he seemed to be struggling to recall recent memories, possibly the last few days or the last few weeks.

"I can't afford to have short-term amnesia, I'm on a case."

She looked up at him again. "What do you remember about it?"

"I've been working on it for weeks. I get to... After this case is solved, I'm transferring."

"You're what? Transferring out of Alaska?"

"Yeah." His voice didn't sound nearly as confident as she would have expected. Just another way that he had changed? Or was he unsure of this decision? She wanted to ask him, but didn't have any right to pry further into his business than she had to because of the situation they were in. If she needed to know something to further assess possible damage from his head injury, she'd ask. Otherwise, she told herself, there was an imaginary line in the sand between the two of them. She wouldn't be the one to cross it. It was unprofessional, and besides, the little she knew about Finn affirmed that the two of them were unlikely to ever be something that could be considered friends. He was too sure of his opinions, confident and inflexible in a way that grated on her. They'd butted heads often during the search for Tori, and they were too different to have any kind of personal relationship.

"So you must really feel pressured to solve this one," she finally said.

"It's not just that. It's…it's similar enough, you know. To Tori's case."

She did know. It had already crossed her mind. Not that that meant it was *that* much like Tori's disappearance in any kind of distinct way. But it reminded her of it.

Tori had been younger, twenty, when she'd gone missing from Eagle Bend. She'd reported last seen leaving her shift at a local coffee shop between Eagle Bend and Soldotna. She'd taken a pedestrian trail that connected the two towns, most of the landscape wilderness. Trees. Long grasses. Swamps. At seven o'clock in the summer, the sun was still high in the sky, but the route was strangely quiet and deserted.

Tori's parents had reported her missing when she didn't come home. The initial police search focused on the area around the coffee shop and pedestrian trail. When they'd gotten an anonymous tip later that a woman matching Tori's description had been seen hiking a boulder field, police searched there…to no avail. Tori had never been found.

All of the women who had disappeared, both in Tori's case and this one, didn't make sense. She'd spoken briefly about her observations about this with the FBI profiler on the case who had told her that often serial killers chose victims who were unlikely to be missed, but that didn't seem to be the case here. The women going missing and winding up dead were productive members of society, people with families. They'd disappeared on hikes, from workplaces, from a grocery store in one instance, one from a walk in her neighborhood. But despite the varied locations where the victims had been last seen, that one thread held them together. They were all buried or hidden in the same general wilderness area. And all of the women had people around them who cared.

People who would be grieved when they disappeared.

Jordyn swallowed hard against her own grief, which people kept telling her would lessen over the years but still seemed almost as fresh as the day she'd learned that Tori had vanished.

"So you do remember this case you're working, though. Details about it?" she asked Finn, forcing herself to stay focused on the present, on *this* conversation.

"I remember everything about it except why I was alone in that mountain pass. I wouldn't have gone up there without backup unless there had been a good reason. And clearly I stepped into something, or I wouldn't have been attacked."

"But you don't remember what you discovered?"

"No. Nor do I remember the attack. But I know it was the killer...in my gut I know I saw the suspect, but I can't remember what they looked like. It's like..." He clenched his eyes shut. "It's like I just lost a day. I remember the day before yesterday, working the case, talking to people at the FBI and the police department...then... I don't think I know anything about yesterday at all."

She studied him. "This may be a crazy idea."

"I'm listening."

"I learned some things about amnesia when I was working on EMT certifications, but I Googled more about it last night. It seems sometimes triggering your memory intentionally could work to recover some of it."

"What did you have in mind? I would think if talking about the case were going to trigger anything, it would have done it already."

"Memory isn't triggered as much by talking as by experiences. What if we go back? To where Cipher and I found you? That's the only place we know you for sure were yesterday, right? So if we go back there, theoretically it could help."

She watched his face as he thought it through. She suspected he must be better at controlling what expressions made it onto his face in everyday life. Surely an FBI agent was supposed to be somewhat hard to read, but at the moment he wasn't. His face was all conflict and indecision, weighing his options.

"I can't ask you to risk that," he finally said, and she blinked back surprise. He'd been debating because of her?

"You're not asking anything of me I didn't offer," she said. "And besides, I have to go back there today anyway."

His eyebrows rose. "Surely that's not safe."

"Nothing about my job is particularly safe. Walking through the woods with a dog looking for missing people?" She laughed a little to try to break the tension, but he didn't smile. Nothing about the seriousness on his face eased at all.

"It's nothing to joke about," he said.

"And you, as an FBI agent, are unfamiliar with dark humor as a coping skill? I obviously don't joke about it because I don't take it seriously. But if we don't joke about it, how else do we handle it?"

"This just isn't an ordinary missing persons case. You realize that, don't you?"

As though because she was SAR and not law enforcement, she was stupid. "The serial killer aspect of it did tip me off there, yes."

He stood. "This isn't funny, Jordyn. People have died. More people are going to die. Someone…someone…" He started to pace, ran a hand through his hair and shook

his head with obvious annoyance. "Someone in law enforcement is involved. Someone from the FBI, I think. It's
just much more dangerous than a normal case. Whoever
is doing this is smart, crazy smart."

Jordyn hurt for him, wished there was a way to help his
frustration. Although there might be, but so far he wasn't
eager to take her up on it. Returning to the scene of whatever had happened to him seemed to her to be the only
way forward.

"I know," she said, taking a deep breath. "So do you want
to go or not?" she asked, for what she planned to be the final
time. His eyes met hers, and he seemed to be considering
it. She felt herself hold her breath, waiting for his answer.

# FOUR

If Finn could have thought of any other way to try to jog his memory than returning to the scene where he'd been attacked, especially with Jordyn, he would have done it. But he'd finally realized as he looked into her eyes that this was the only option he had. He was thankful to her, but the idea of endangering her any more than he already had...he didn't have to like it. At all.

"You feeling okay?" she asked him as they climbed into her SUV. They'd cleaned up and eaten breakfast, and Jordyn had had coffee—he hadn't felt good enough to try coffee with this kind of headache—after he'd agreed to her offer, and they'd done so in relative silence. He didn't know what to say, everything was overwhelming at the moment. He found himself grateful for his lack of memories about yesterday. At least he didn't have to worry about recalling what must have been an incredibly disconcerting experience, not knowing who he was.

His current state was irritating enough. To be relatively certain that he had most, if not all, of the puzzle pieces he needed to wrap up this serial killer case and still be stuck in the middle of it for a reason as frustrating as that his brain had stopped working...it was maddening.

"Finn?" It wasn't until he heard Jordyn's voice again that

he remembered she'd asked him a question. Was he okay? How did he answer that?

"I'm fine." He went with the standard answer to a question like that, one that everyone knew could mean anything you wanted it to.

The look she shot him told him that she knew better, but she didn't say anything to directly contradict his deflection, which he appreciated. Sometimes it just didn't feel like the time to get into something.

They pulled into the parking lot at the trailhead, and Finn saw his car at the edge of the lot, abandoned. There was something eerie in knowing you'd functionally disappeared, that no one knew where you were or if you were okay. Except you. And a woman you barely knew. He'd checked his phone—nothing from anyone who knew him on a personal level, though there weren't many people who'd qualify for that category anyway. His parents had their own lives in Seattle, having moved there not long after tragedy rocked their family. They wouldn't notice him missing, not right away. His friends were all part of the job—less friends than coworkers. There were several texts from people at work asking if he was okay, but he couldn't respond. Not without possibly alerting the killer to the fact that he was still alive.

He pulled his mind back to the present. Jordyn was watching him take in the scene, he could tell. Which told him that she was observant. Probably good at her job if they had her assigned to this serial killer case. It was a little surprising that they hadn't run into each other yet, other than that Finn did generally try to stay out of the way of dog handlers and the K-9s they worked with. He knew plenty of people who had a story of a case they'd only had solved because of a dog, but he wasn't entirely convinced that other search methods and processes of investigation weren't as effective, if slightly less glamorous. Putting that much faith into an animal…it made him uneasy. Then again, Finn didn't like to put faith into anyone besides himself.

There was no one else in the lot, but Finn appreciated that Jordyn hesitated before she opened her door to make sure there was no one else they could see, anyway.

Not that that meant there was no one around. There was a cluster of trees in the distance. Anyone could be hiding in those trees. While the killer's MO so far was a handgun at close range, at this point anything could happen. The killer could be trying to eliminate the threat at all costs. Finn did his best to stay alert, watch for any telltale glints in the morning sun that could indicate a rifle scope, but saw nothing.

Was it safe? Or just quiet? He'd learned long ago that the two were not the same.

"I thought we'd take Cipher, hike back to show you where I found you yesterday, and then if you think it's okay, you can come with me while I search some of this grid I was working on yesterday. No one else is assigned to the spot we are headed, and no one knows about you disappearing, so we should be the only ones there."

"Sounds good." His head was fuzzy. He appreciated that she'd thought it out, but it grated on him that he didn't feel like he could reason things out as well as usual. It was like his brain was wrapped in some kind of thick fog, like a white blanket pressing on him when he tried to think. He rubbed his head.

"You're really sure you're up to this?" she asked.

"My head hurts, and it's just hard to think. It's annoying."

"Head injuries do that. Give it time, you'll see improvements if you don't overdo it. I'm not a doctor, but I do think this hike is worth the risk. Then we'll get you back to my house, let you rest."

Rest didn't sound as terrible as he wished it did.

Jordyn let her dog out of the car, and Cipher looked up at her, locking eyes with her handler like all she wanted was to make her happy. He didn't have to be fully confident in the abilities of search dogs to see that this was a special animal. Maybe there was something to her skills after all. He'd have to see.

They set off following the dog. The trees were thick, mostly dark-colored Sitka spruce of various heights. They were thick enough to obscure the sun in some places, making the woods darker than the surrounding area, which added to Finn's general sense of unease.

Jordyn didn't look uncomfortable in the slightest. Her head was up as she alternated between watching her dog and looking around, sweeping both sides of the trail and woods with her eyes. They hadn't spent much time together when they were younger. As a rule, Finn had avoided his sister's friends. Probably because he could remember the fallout when he hadn't avoided Tori's friend once, in middle school, and she'd gotten a crush on him. The drama that had ensued had been of the typical middle school variety, but the worst fallout from it was that Tori had been hurt when her friend didn't want to be friends anymore. He'd sworn then not to get involved with his sister's friends anymore and had taken himself seriously enough that when Jordyn had moved to town in Tori's early high school years and the two of them had become inseparable, he'd stayed far away from her.

He'd noticed her, though. She was funny, brave and altogether more attractive to him than he wanted one of his sister's friends to be.

So he'd stayed even further away, and had probably been borderline rude to her in an effort to stay distanced. Tori had tried to talk to him about it, but he wouldn't listen. Nothing had been worth risking his sister's happiness or their relationship.

Did Jordyn know about all that? He wondered now as they walked through the woods. Did he owe her any kind of explanation, or should he just let her think he was stand-offish and rude?

"It's pretty far in here," Jordyn said, turning back to him and pulling him from his thoughts.

"How did you get me out?" he asked, not remembering if he'd asked already, or if he had, what the answer had been.

"You walked, actually. I thought I was going to have to figure out some kind of way to build a sled with branches and pull you, but you regained just enough consciousness to walk out with my arm around you."

Was it his imagination, or had she looked away when she said the last part? Maybe she felt weird about this situation too. It wasn't like they'd been close and relying on each other was normal for them. But it also wasn't the same as helping out a total stranger. Their lack of close history was in itself sort of a form of history, wasn't it?

"I'm glad you didn't have to figure out how to do that," he finally said. "I'm sorry for all of this."

"For something entirely out of your control?"

"For dragging you into it."

"Again, entirely out of your control."

"Maybe, but…"

She stopped walking, turned to face him. "I could have

walked away. I didn't. So I'm in this intentionally, all right? No more apologies."

Her eyes flickered with emotion, but she met his gaze unflinchingly.

"Okay," he finally said. "No apologies."

She turned back around, her long red ponytail swishing as she did so. "Another mile," she said.

His head ached as he followed the narrow trail, but no worse than it had. Then Cipher cut left, into the woods.

Jordyn frowned. "We didn't go this way yesterday. Weird that the scent would be stronger this way? If she's following the same trail…" She took off after the dog, not waiting for Finn's response. He quickened his pace to keep up. Jordyn wasn't running, but she wasn't walking at a casual pace anymore either. He may not know a lot about working with K-9s, but he could tell there'd been some kind of shift in momentum. They'd been casually walking toward wherever Jordyn had found him yesterday, and now they were following the dog's intuition.

It was odd, to say the least, but he had to admit, impressive. At least, if this turned up anything new.

Cipher seemed to know what she was doing.

"Okay, wait, this is the same clearing up ahead where you were," Jordyn called back.

He waited for some bit of recognition as they stepped from the darkness of the trees into the sunlit clearing but found nothing.

Pushing past his frustration, Finn took a breath and decided to think about it like it was a case. One he was new to. Look around, make observations, try to see the scene as it unfolded…his training came to the forefront as he worked to get his emotions under control.

It was a clearing in the middle of the woods, and there

was green everywhere. The ground cover was green, bushes and brush that from far away would make it look like a low clearing when really it was a tangle of weeds. That might yield something, if there were spots that seemed trampled or worn down more than others. He'd have to see.

Beyond that, there wasn't much unique about it. It looked like many other isolated clearings in the Alaskan wilderness, the spruce trees and brush the hallmark of this part of the Kenai Peninsula.

Cipher was crossing the space, leaving a subtle trail through the brush, and then she stopped a little more than halfway through. Lay down and howled.

"That looks like right about where she found you," Jordyn said. "Come with me, we'll stay in her trail."

Not used to being the one to take orders, he still did what she said, stepping carefully even as he looked at the ground on either side of the trail, looking for anything that could give him something to work with. Had whoever had attacked him dropped anything, left any trace? What had happened here in this clearing that had made someone want to attack him, anyway? If he'd been in the woods, maybe he'd seen something? But then why had he been in the clearing?

Jordyn had stopped next to Cipher and was kneeling down beside her.

"Is that where I was?" he asked.

She shook her head. "Almost. But… I don't think so. No. Three more feet to the right, maybe?" She motioned to the right, and Finn could see depressions in the brush that seemed to fit.

But beside Cipher, where Jordyn was kneeling, there were other beaten-down bushes, like something had been lying there, or dragged there.

Or both.

"Is that…" He stepped forward, about to move closer, before he realized this was more Jordyn's scene than his, and he didn't want to mess up something he didn't know to be looking for. "Can I kneel down next to you?" he asked.

Jordyn nodded without looking away from the plant she was studying.

Along the brown-and-green stem of the large plant was a rust-colored streak. And more across a few leaves on the ground.

"Blood," he finally said aloud. "And not mine?"

"You were farther that way," she said again. "And while it's not impossible… That isn't Cipher's alert for a live human. It's the same one she used yesterday, when we found you. It's her human remains alert."

"But I'm alive," he said, stating the obvious.

She looked up, met his eyes. "But I'm starting to think that someone else was with you and your attacker. And that that person was not."

# FIVE

If there had been any doubt in Finn's mind that he was attacked in connection with the serial killer case he'd been on, it disappeared with Jordyn's comment.

"So Cipher wasn't confused," Jordyn continued. "I was glad she found you, but it was strange that she alerted as though you were a body. But she didn't. She alerted to the smells of human remains in this spot."

"Does she search for live people too, or only deceased?"

"Live. But it's a different alert. I'd asked her to search for bodies yesterday because I was supposed to be searching this grid for the serial killer's latest presumed victim." Jordyn was still kneeling. She photographed the indentions in the brush. After a few minutes, she looked up at Finn.

"I need to tell my boss," she said.

"About what?"

"This blood. This was the grid I was given to search, and he needs to know that Cipher alerted on a spot that had a dead body. This confirms that the latest missing woman is almost certainly another victim of this serial killer."

He didn't want to stop her from doing her job, and he certainly didn't want to stand in the way of justice being brought, but that didn't change the way his chest tightened when she talked about bringing law enforcement in to what she had discovered. He still felt slightly disoriented, and his headache was worsening in the wake of this new discovery.

He needed to make a decision. Yesterday, he had told Jordyn not to take him for medical care because he'd been convinced it wouldn't be safe. She'd said it seemed he didn't trust the FBI.

That distrust, the deep anxiety, was still there. Something wasn't right. His gut told him not to inform the police or the Bureau. But did that mean he was going to disappear entirely? That was the only way to do it, to fall off the grid, let the FBI assume he'd been taken out by the serial killer as well.

Otherwise whoever had attacked him was likely going to finish what they'd started. While he didn't want to stop working on the case, he didn't see that he had much of an option other than to lie low and evade the attacker. Going back to work could mean tipping the killer off to his whereabouts. He couldn't do the case or anyone else any good if he was dead.

"I need to know that you won't tell your boss that you found me," he said.

"Still? I thought maybe since you had some of your memory back now..."

"Some. I still don't know who was responsible for attacking me or why."

"But how are you going to find out without resources? Where are you going to go? What's your plan?"

He stood. Walked away from the scene a little and looked up at the sky. The clouds were thick today, making the green of the mountainside seem even deeper and more vibrant. The clouds were low, mist hung in the air and the entire scene was something otherworldly, almost out of a fairy tale.

Except something darker hung in the air here as well. The awareness that someone had been murdered in this meadow tainted it somehow, discordant among the beauty of Alaskan summer. A nagging at the edge of Finn's mind added to his sense of unease. If he'd been here, if he'd seen something…why couldn't he remember it?

His sister would have told him to pray about it. Strange that he could think about Tori and it was almost normal not to see her. It seemed like a lifetime ago that she'd been alive, since he'd last spoken to her. How could that be possible when at the same time it seemed fresh, a sharp jolt of grief surprising him out of the blue when he couldn't just call her up.

Praying had been Tori's default. Good news? She prayed and thanked God for it. Bad news? She'd talked to God about it, sometimes asking Him to change her circumstances, sometimes asking for help understanding. And Finn had prayed too. At one point.

When God didn't answer your prayers to save your sister from a madman? It was tough to pray after that.

Slamming that door shut in his mind, he moved back to where Jordyn had stood from her investigation of the bloodstained flora.

"I don't know what my plan is," he said as he approached, shaking his head, struggling with the answer to the questions she'd asked him. They were good questions, well thought out and necessary to consider. "I just know that someone tried to kill me, and if I walk back into the FBI office, the chances are good they're going to succeed."

"Someone there? In the FBI?"

He considered, tried to force the information out of the recesses of his brain, and then when that didn't work, he tried to relax his brain to see if maybe the information would present itself if he sort of…caught it unawares.

No…nothing. He still couldn't remember. But the FBI specifically made him feel uneasy. Strange, since he loved his job and the people he worked with. "Yeah. Someone there. I'm pretty sure. Or with the police department, maybe." He raked a hand through his hair. "I hear how ridiculous it sounds though, and I'm not sure enough to accuse anyone of anything. I don't see how someone there would be involved. Unless somehow someone is leaking information to the killer or…" He trailed off, shook his head. "I don't know. I just know my gut is telling me not to go back right now, and since my brain doesn't appear to be at full capacity, I'm going to trust my instincts for now." The last part had only come to him just now, as he was talking, but it made just as much sense as anything.

"How? Are you…" She trailed off like she was weighing her words, and her eyes seemed to be assessing him as her voice paused. "Do you want my help?"

"No, you've done enough. I can't ask you for that."

Even as he said it, Finn knew his options were limited, though. How was he supposed to find somewhere to hide out if it wasn't at Jordyn's house? He couldn't exactly return to his old apartment without repercussions—like a coworker coming to check on him once the FBI realized he was missing—and renting a new place would be next to impossible without using his ID. If this were an undercover FBI operation and he'd been compromised somehow, they'd handle keeping him safe. What was he supposed to do when he was pretty sure the threat was from within?

"I don't think you have a choice," she said.

He didn't. But it still grated that she knew that.

He shrugged. "Then maybe I'll go back to the FBI and

hope I'm wrong. But I'm not going to do that to you. I've put you in enough danger already."

"I put myself in danger. You didn't force me to take you home."

"It's still not fair to ask, not when we barely know each other, and you don't even…" He'd said more than he should have.

"I don't even what?"

"You don't even like me. I'm not someone you should be risking your life for."

"Where do I start with that?" Her eyes flashed something like fire in his direction. "Like I'd only risk myself for people I like? Basically against everything I do in my job and kind of insulting."

"I didn't mean for it to be. I do have a concussion, you know. I'm not going to explain all this right."

"That's true." Her facial expression softened a little. "Okay, I'll let the offended thing go, even though, to be clear, what you said was definitely offensive."

It had been. She wasn't wrong. "Thanks. I appreciate it."

"And another thing, I don't dislike you."

That didn't exactly explain why he'd always felt like she did, but he'd have to take her word for it.

"I think I'm your best option here," she said. "Come back to my house. Hole up in the cabin for a few days, weeks, whatever you think, and then hopefully this will all be in the past, and the killer will be brought to justice."

It could drag on longer than that. They both knew it from experience. From the days that had turned to weeks, then months, without any new developments in his sister's case. Years of silence and no new information.

"For now," he said softly, "I think that's my best option. If you're sure it's a risk you're willing to take." He wasn't convinced his presence wouldn't bring more danger to her doorstep, but the intruder had seen her today. There was nothing guaranteeing whoever was after him wouldn't come back to get rid of her next.

"I'm sure," she affirmed. "Ready to head back?"

He was and they started off together. Even though it was only midday, it seemed slightly dimmer outside than it had even that morning. Logically, he knew it was only because of the way the sun had dipped behind an even thicker cloud and not as much light was reaching them.

Psychologically, he felt like the dimming was some kind of sign. Things were going to get darker before they got light again.

He only hoped finding the truth in this case didn't cost either of them any more than it already had.

Finn had been too quiet on the hike back, and he was quiet again on the drive home. It bothered Jordyn to some degree that they'd known each other for years and didn't know each other at all. Yet how was she supposed to do anything about that if the man wouldn't talk?

Of course, when he did talk, much more spilled out than she was expecting. Who would have guessed that he thought she didn't like him at all? She'd avoided him as a teen, but it was only because it would have been entirely too easy to develop a crush on her best friend's older brother. It was a cliché for a reason, and the first time Jordyn had seen Finn at school, before she'd realized he was Tori's brother, she'd thought he was cute.

As soon as she realized the two were related, she stuck any possible feelings she could have developed for him in the back of her mind and unofficially vowed not to act on them. More than once she'd wondered, her senior year, if maybe she wasn't the only one who might be attracted, and if it wasn't such a bad idea with disaster written all over it…but then college had taken them their separate ways, and Tori's disappearance had separated them even further. Their disagreements hadn't just been over how to handle the search, if law enforcement or SAR teams should be trusted more, they'd been over everything. Jordyn had wanted to get involved in the search as a civilian volunteer and had, yet Finn had thought it was too dangerous. It seemed to her sometimes like if she had one opinion, he had another.

Now she wondered how much of that was because they were so fundamentally different as people and how much was because they were both stressed, devastated, grieving over someone they'd cared about.

Either way, reuniting with him in this way was far from comfortable. Finn was right that this situation wasn't ideal. No, he hadn't said that specifically, but it had been implied, and she was not going to argue that. But she didn't see any other alternative, and she certainly wasn't going to let Tori's brother be murdered just because the idea of hiding him— of getting involved in this investigation, of letting *anyone* into her quiet, well-ordered life—brought her to the brink of a panic attack. She'd figure out how to handle this, get through it and then move on. It was what she did.

It was what she'd *always* done.

Part of her wanted to dive into the *why* of that, why she kept people at arm's length and if it was a natural part of growing up or if it was as a result of losing her best friend in the violent way she had. She wished she could analyze herself the way she would have a case study in college. She loved considering why people did the things they did, how they interacted; it was what had drawn her to psychology in the first place.

She'd barely gotten to study it before reality had pulled her away. Studying people didn't do nearly as much good as learning to train dogs, being on the SAR team. Because people had a flaw—they were fundamentally broken. And once Tori had disappeared, it had been a lot more difficult for Jordyn to reconcile herself to the idea that maybe they could still be fixed. Mended.

She knew the right answers, of course. Her parents had made sure she was in Sunday school as a kid every week, and even now, with all that she'd seen, Jordyn didn't doubt that God could change people's hearts and behaviors.

But she also knew that He gave people choices. And some of them seemed to persist in making the wrong ones no matter how many second, third or fourth chances you gave them.

Jordyn pulled into her driveway and parked the car, and they all went inside. She gave Cipher a bone to chew when they got home. She could tell that the last twenty-four hours were weighing on her. Human remains dogs fascinated her—at least as much as human psychology did, if not more. Though K-9s were trained to alert on human remains and it was "good" when they did so, it also seemed to affect them deeply. On an emotional level.

Dogs understood death, and it hurt them, the way it seemed to hurt everyone.

She didn't want Cipher to struggle with the weight of that any more than their job dictated, so she did her best to take the strain off where she could, to reward Cipher for her finds, to keep spirits light, to make sure the dog didn't spiral into anxiety.

On the couch, Finn had laid down to take a nap. She had so many more questions for him, but she'd forced herself not to ask them all at once. It was obvious that just com-

ing up with a general plan for how he was going to manage his "disappearance" had taken a lot out of him, and he
was still recovering from a head injury. She didn't want to
push him too far.

For now, she was going to head into town and talk to her
boss. She'd considered calling him, but she wanted to see
his face when she talked to him. Finn's suspicions seemed
to land on someone working for the FBI, but Jordyn wasn't
taking any chances. She needed to know she could trust
Sergeant Patrick, and she was fairly certain she could. This
would hopefully confirm that.

Plus, she thought it might be wise to see what the general conversation in town was, especially in law enforcement circles, about Finn's disappearance. She didn't know
how long he'd been missing when she found him, but she
didn't think it had been long, given how hurt he'd been and
how rapidly he'd improved since then.

Leaving Finn asleep and unprotected made her uncomfortable, but the trip to town couldn't be avoided. For now
she had to hope that the killer was still unaware that Finn
was alive, that maybe she had been the target of the break-in
earlier. But just in case, she left Cipher. The dog would protect him as well or better than Jordyn could.

Jordyn drove into town without incident and parked
in front of the Eagle Bend Police Department. The parking lot was even fuller than it had been over the last few
weeks, which was substantially fuller than usual. Most of
the time this was a fairly quiet town, but when something
happened, it was often big. Alaska gave the impression of
being paradise on earth, and Jordyn thought it was close,
but when crime did happen it was often a serious crime.
Alaska's violent crime rankings were nothing to brag about
and were something she wished she had an inkling of how

to fix. Looking around, she wondered how many FBI agents would be here today. It wasn't unusual for them to come and go lately from the police department, as they'd been looped into the investigation as soon as it had become obvious there was a serial killer involved. It was standard operating procedure for the FBI to be called in when a police department realized that a pattern of deaths made a serial killer likely. Sometimes it was for extra manpower in the form of agents, who they'd had some help from—so it was a little surprising that Jordyn hadn't seen Finn around. Then again, she spent as little time here at the police department as possible. Technically she wasn't employed by the PD; she was an independent contractor, so she was mostly able to avoid the low-ceilinged brown building and spend most of her time outside instead. She didn't like coming into town much at all, really, preferring to keep to herself at her house or out in the woods.

In addition to extra manpower, police departments involved in serial killer cases often made use of an FBI profiler. Melissa Reynolds, the profiler on this case, was tall, blond and always put together. Jordyn had worked with her briefly when they were discussing the highest priority grids for her and Cipher to search, but that was it. She'd only had minimal interaction with the FBI agents on the case. Agent Hawkins had accompanied her on a search once, but the tall, dark and entirely too silent agent had made her uncomfortable somehow, probably because he was so intensely quiet, and she'd mostly searched on her own since then.

"Morning." She nodded to Bella Hall at the front desk.

"Good morning." Bella smiled back, but Jordyn thought it might have looked like a tighter smile than usual. "Sergeant Patrick was hoping you might be by today. Any news?"

"Nothing too solid." She avoided answering with specifics. She didn't usually guard information so carefully, but right now no one felt particularly safe, especially when she didn't know who might overhear.

No wonder Finn wanted—no, *needed*—to disappear right now. If he didn't, how on earth would he be able to function and do his job?

"You can go on back anyway. He'll be glad to see you." Bella smiled again then reached for the ringing phone to answer it.

It didn't take her long to make her way to Sergeant Patrick's office. This wasn't a large department by any means, so the building felt cramped at the moment. Every available space was being used, and their small interrogation room was now serving as a break room so that the regular break room could be turned into a command center. It made for a strange atmosphere when you were getting coffee, being in a room that had been intentionally designed to be uncomfortable, but they were making it work.

If Sergeant Patrick wasn't in his office, he might be in the command center talking to other officers who were working the case. She hoped that wouldn't be the situation. This was difficult enough, to give him the information she needed to pass on without being suspicious or letting on that she knew anything about Finn's disappearance.

For a brief moment, she wondered if she should have avoided checking in, if telling him about the blood was that important, when the woman was clearly beyond their help now. But no, obviously she needed to tell him. Her family deserved closure, for one thing. For another, every single clue that put them one step closer to finding who was behind this mattered. It had to. Because every clue made it more likely that the killer would slip, that they'd discover a pattern. That eventually there wouldn't be a "next victim."

So she took a deep breath and walked into the room.

# SIX

Sergeant Patrick was sitting at his desk. Jordyn felt her shoulders relax, just slightly, as she walked into the room. At least she didn't have to try to have this conversation with an audience. She shut the door behind her.

His eyebrows rose. She didn't usually shut the door, as she'd never had a reason to try to restrict who was privy to the information she shared. Sergeant Patrick had gotten to where he was by noticing details, so of course he'd noticed this one.

"Everything okay, Jordyn? Have a seat." He motioned to the matching blue chairs in front of his desk, and she sat in one of them. She leaned forward, trying to process how she was going to explain this while telling the truth and not giving away anything about Finn.

Technically Sergeant Patrick had no reason to connect them, but did anyone know where Finn had disappeared *from*? His car was still at the trailhead. If he had a point last seen that put him in her search grid, someone might ask.

She wasn't going to lie for him. Her integrity and her job were both important enough to her that she wasn't interested in doing the wrong thing for the right reasons. That wasn't who she was.

But Jordyn also couldn't deny that it seemed to her that

Finn's logic was solid. If, despite his memory loss, he was convinced that someone at the FBI knew more than they were letting on, were tied to the killer somehow, then they absolutely couldn't know that he'd gotten away. Especially, she realized now, since no one but her knew that he'd lost his memory.

"Everything's fine," she said calmly, attempting to slow her now racing heartbeat. "I mean, you know…" She let the sentence hang, unfinished.

"It's been a tough case for everyone, but if it's too difficult for you…" Sergeant Patrick trailed off. She whipped her head up to meet his eyes, then realized he wasn't trying to get her off the case or doubting her abilities. In fact, he looked genuinely concerned.

"Too difficult?" she repeated, hoping he'd say more.

"The last few months, the longer this has dragged on, the more I've wondered if this hits too close to home for you. I know you've worked a variety of cases in the years you've been contracted with the department, but women disappearing at the hands of a serial killer…it's just not the kind of thing that happens around here often, and the last time you knew the victim, correct?"

Jordyn nodded. "I did. But this isn't the same, and it's not too difficult for me. I'm fine."

He studied her for a minute, then nodded. "If it's not that, what's going on?"

His eyes flicked to the closed door.

"I may have found something. Well, Cipher did. We were searching our grid yesterday and today—" she did her best to keep her voice casual, to elicit no suspicion "—and this morning we found a spot with dried blood."

"A lot?"

"Enough." She shook her head. "Of course I can't prove

anything, that's for someone else to look into, but I suspect it's going to be significant to the case."

"Where?" He slid out a map of the search grid, and she leaned over the desk, showed him the location.

Sergeant Patrick looked up and met her eyes briefly before looking back down at the map. "You know," he started, "the FBI lost a man around there yesterday. He'd headed there on some kind of hunch and then disappeared. Allegedly." He frowned. "Maybe you should stay home for a day or two, it might not be worth the risk."

She took a deep breath. So they knew that Finn was missing. That was good. It meant that he might have a few days to regroup, figure out who was after him, without them being after him directly. That was, assuming that the break-in at her house had been the killer coming after her and not him.

Either way, neither of them could afford to relax.

"I don't want to compromise the search or slow anything down," she said, hoping he wouldn't bench her. It was true that the danger had escalated, and one of the things she'd learned in her search and rescue training was that searchers were supposed to be kept reasonably safe. As important as what they did was, they couldn't run SAR organizations if they routinely let SAR workers step unprotected into unreasonable amounts of danger.

"Do they think it's connected? I mean, are they thinking he's a victim or a person of interest?" she asked.

He shook his head. "Too soon to say. The profiler is supposed to be talking to us all this afternoon with an update from the last few days, what movements could mean, her thoughts on all of this. That meeting was scheduled before he was reported missing, so could be unrelated. I know they're searching for him, though. I've got to get ready for that, so unless there's something else…" The way his voice trailed off was a dismissal that Jordyn was only too happy to listen to. She'd avoided lying, which was a win, and had delivered the information she needed to. She moved to the door and eased it open.

"If he's a person of interest—did you know him well enough to give any kind of statement or interview?" he asked as she was stepping out.

"Who was it?" she asked, at the last minute realizing that he hadn't given her a name and answering before he'd told her would let Sergeant Patrick know that she knew more than she was letting on.

"Finn McDaniel. You know him, right?"

Something about the way he was watching her had her wondering if he suspected she knew information she wasn't sharing. If he knew she'd rescued Finn. Could he have seen them somehow? She searched her mind but couldn't find any reason he'd know anything.

She shrugged. "Barely knew him when we were teens. I only knew him through Tori."

"You haven't seen him recently?"

"We lost contact after I moved." She shrugged again. "I wouldn't have pegged him for a killer, though."

"Let me know if you see him. Understand?"

"Yes, sir. I understand." She smiled then walked back out.

She blew out an enormous breath as she made her way down the hallway, feeling a bit like someone who was barely escaping from a trap. Not that she thought Sergeant Patrick was trapping her. At least, she didn't *think* so? It was difficult to know who to trust at this point.

"Something wrong?"

The smooth voice of Melissa Reynolds, the FBI profiler,

startled Jordyn enough that she jumped, then tried to play it off with a laugh. Probably pretty unsuccessfully. "Wow, you scared me."

The two other agents Melissa had been talking to—Agent Hawkins and Agent Littleton—moved away, as though to give them a chance to talk in private. Jordyn didn't know either of them well but knew the FBI had quite a few people working on this case currently.

"Oh?" Melissa raised her eyebrows, and Jordyn had the impression she was being studied. Two people in one morning—she was starting to wish she'd stayed home and sent the sergeant a text. "Tense morning?"

"No more than it has been for these last few weeks." Jordyn shook her head.

"Oh?"

Jordyn sort of hated the way the other woman had the tendency to use the word *oh* to probe into people's minds. Of course, she wasn't especially predisposed to being tolerant about being studied this morning either. Being noticed was the last thing she wanted today. Her goal had been to get in and get out while engaging with other people as little as possible. It felt like Melissa was studying her. As a suspect? As a human she wanted to analyze?

"It's a stressful job sometimes," she said in an even voice, deciding that engaging with her was more likely to end this encounter sooner. If she kept avoiding conversation, the profiler was just going to dig deeper. It was probably an occupational hazard, where people changed the way they interacted even with people they weren't supposed to be analyzing. "But it always works out." She offered a small smile.

"Let me know if you need to talk. I want to be here for

anyone who needs that." Melissa smiled back and Jordyn nodded.

"I will. Thanks."

Without breaking her stride, Jordyn headed for the door. She needed to get back to her house, hopefully before Finn woke up.

And hopefully, definitely, before anyone realized he was there.

"You okay, Jordyn?"

Of course she was stopped again. It was Officer Lee, one of the Eagle Bend police officers she'd worked with before. Lee was good. She had transferred into their department from Anchorage, and Jordyn always got the sense there was more to her than met the eye. She was a competent police officer, but there always seemed to be just a little more to her that Jordyn had always wondered about. She'd love to know the woman's story sometime.

"Yeah, fine. Definitely fine."

"Did you hear one of the FBI agents went missing?"

Could no one talk about anything besides Finn? Yes, it was an understandable thing to fixate on, but there were plenty of other aspects of the case Jordyn would have preferred to discuss.

"I did. Any idea what happened to him?" she asked, hoping she sounded substantially more casual than she felt.

Officer Lee shook her head. "No, you?"

Jordyn laughed. Definitely not a casual laugh. Probably a nervous laugh.

She cleared her throat. "No. I wish I knew." And she did. So it wasn't entirely a lie.

Now Lee was studying her. Something about the way she narrowed her eyes made Jordyn curious if she knew more than she was letting on. Finn was so sure he couldn't trust law enforcement, and the FBI and Eagle Bend Police Department were working closely together. Would it necessarily be an FBI agent who could be leaking information to a killer accidentally, or worse, could *be* the killer? Or was every officer in Eagle Bend a suspect too? Jordyn wasn't sure.

"I've really got to go," Jordyn finally said, not quite making eye contact. Officer Lee didn't say anything else, but the way she was watching her was unnerving. Eerie.

Finally, Jordyn made it to the front door and the parking lot.

She hurried to the car, looking around as unobtrusively as she could in the parking lot for anything suspicious. She didn't know why, but being at the police department had just made all of this more real to her. This had been a safe place, always. Even during the tumultuous times surrounding Tori's disappearance, she'd been able to count on the people in this building. And maybe she still could, she reminded herself as she navigated her car down the road, but with Finn's attack and his insistence it was someone connected to the FBI… That didn't mean any of her police department coworkers were linked. But the knowledge that someone was hiding something made her uncomfortable.

Her house was only about fifteen minutes away from the police department, so at least she should be home quickly. They could talk and regroup.

# SEVEN

She'd noticed the potential problem maybe three miles from town, and Jordyn knew she was the only one to blame that she hadn't noticed earlier. After leaving the police station, she'd been distracted, something she should have known better than to let happen. There was a car behind her when she glanced in the rearview mirror. It was a light blue Subaru, and it was following just a little more closely than she was comfortable with. The driver, from her quick glances in the rearview, appeared to be wearing a dark-colored baseball cap.

An unsettling weight shifted in her stomach. Jordyn accelerated slightly, hoping she could go faster than the other car. Well, really she was hoping that the car had nothing to do with her, and they'd stay slow, and Jordyn would make it back to her house safely and find Finn safely napping on the couch or maybe awakened with his memory back.

But that seemed like a stretch. For now, it was enough to hope that she was just being paranoid, that the car had nothing to do with her or the information she'd given the sergeant or anything she'd seen.

When she accelerated slightly again, the Subaru sped up.

Unfortunately, Jordyn was all too aware that her options were limited. This was Moose River; there weren't a lot of extra roads or places to try to lose a tail, not that she really knew how to do that anyway. But in a city, maybe she'd have tried. As it was, there was really only one way to her house, and it was down the main highway that went straight through the middle of town then down several winding roads that led through spruce forest and muskeg swamp.

If she had to run away at some point, it would have to be on foot.

Who knew where that thought had come from. Hopefully she was borrowing trouble. She didn't usually have to think like this, in a way that felt tactical, organized. She was search and rescue, not law enforcement. And while it wasn't the first time she'd felt unsafe while working a case, it was the first time the consequences had seemed this dire, that the stakes had been quite so *high*.

All she had to do was make it home. Then she'd lock the doors and be safe.

The car was still behind her. Her only option was to go home and risk the person following her. Anything she had to protect herself with, whether it was Cipher or a weapon or even bear spray, was at her house. Home was really the only logical option.

As she approached the one-lane road over the river, she realized her next error, which was forgetting that this spot existed on the way to her house. The road narrowed due to the small bridge, and the Moose River ran lazily underneath. It was a huge liability in a dangerous situation.

Another glance at the rearview mirror. The Subaru was gaining on her. No way could someone tailing her this aggressively not mean harm. Ditch the car and run? Pulling a U-turn wasn't an option. Hit the gas and hope she was fast enough to reach the relative safety of the other side?

She was still deciding when she felt the first impact as

the Subaru rammed into her back end, the sound of metal crunching like a shudder in her stomach as she jolted forward. The sound, the impact, sent chills down her spine.

Jordyn hit the gas hard, deciding that was the safest way to go, especially if the person behind her came at her again. Who was it? Surely not the killer…wouldn't it be too risky to go after her in broad daylight? Besides, Jordyn didn't know anything. The discovery of the blood where she'd found Finn wasn't important enough for this, was it? Her car lurched forward, but not quite fast enough. The Subaru had hit the gas too, side swiping her near the left rear tire and sending her spinning out of control toward the edge of the bridge. The scrape of the metal guardrail against the car made her shudder, but Jordyn had never been so thankful for a guardrail. The river was slow and tame by Alaska standards, but the water was still cold and fairly rapid. She'd still be exposed, if the car crashed and she had to leave it and flee on foot.

Her relief was short-lived. Though she'd managed to narrowly avoid being taken out on the bridge, the final ramming that the Subaru did sent Jordyn off the road and into the tall grasses that encroached on the side of the road. Much further forward and she'd have hit trees because on this stretch of road it was like the forest was trying to take over. As it was, the grass was bad enough. Her tires caught in ruts she couldn't see, threw her to the side, and she came to an abrupt stop in what she assumed from the bumping was muskeg swamp—a low-lying area where soft, squishy ground was punctuated every few feet by hard clumps of dirt with grass growing out of them. She was stuck.

And the car was pulling in behind her.

Jordyn didn't wait to see who was behind the wheel, as the knowledge wouldn't do her any good if she was dead.

Instead she ran, realizing quickly that she'd been right about the terrain. Tussocks, clumps of solid ground that stood like tiny hills all over the swampy ground, made it uneven and difficult to run. Lost footing would be disastrous here, something as simple as a rolled ankle having the potential to turn deadly with someone on her heels.

After a minute or two of running, she finally looked back, hoping to see that she'd overreacted. The person from the car was following her. Footsteps pounded behind her, getting closer and closer. Jordyn didn't register any details about the pursuer besides the black streak of movement in the corner of her eye, but it was enough to confirm that she had to keep running. Her life depended on it.

She trampled through the underbrush, pushing herself faster.

Her phone was in her pocket. That was something, at least, though she couldn't risk stopping to use it right now. Police response time in Moose River was better than in some cities—after all, the town wasn't that big geographically—but it still wouldn't be enough. She'd have to get away on her own to have a chance.

She ran, careful of her footing as she splashed through the swampy land, wondering if the other victims had run too. And Tori, so many years ago. Had they felt this awful feeling of inevitability? It had Jordyn long to live even more, not just for her own sake, but so she could bring the killers in both sets of crimes to justice. No one should ever have to feel this way.

Deep in the spruce woods, out of the swamp, she finally slowed down, glanced back again, and this time saw nothing.

She'd searched these woods before, she realized as she looked around. A missing kid who'd gotten lost from his backyard and had been found in the woods, not far from where she was now. He'd taken shelter near a stand of fallen spruce, and Jordyn remembered how difficult it had been for Cipher to get to where the boy had been hidden between the branches. She'd never have seen him herself if it hadn't been for Cipher's nose and abilities. With that in mind, she headed for where she remembered the trees being and found them less than a minute later. Jordyn hesitated slightly. If she was wrong, if this wasn't as good a hiding spot as she thought, it could cost her her life. Maybe Finn's too because he certainly wasn't going to sit still when she didn't return as planned, was he?

Making a split-second decision, she wriggled her way through the branches, scratching her upper arm on one of the protruding spruces. The sting pulsed in tempo with her heart rate as she crawled as deep into the thicket as she could go.

Hopefully this was enough. Hopefully Finn... What? What did she want him to do? He'd been asleep when she'd left. Suffering from a head injury. What she'd better hope was that no one found her, and that Finn also stayed right where he was. There was no need for both of them to be in the path of a killer.

The woods were thick and dark. The trees choked out all but a thin layer of sunlight. Finn felt his shoulders tense. Maybe Finn had underestimated how it would feel to return to the woods alone after what had happened the other day.

As though thinking about it made it worse, he felt a stab of pain in his head. He pressed on anyway, following Cipher's lead, feeling more and more ridiculous the farther he walked. Not that he thought his instincts were wrong about Jordyn being in trouble. He was convinced something had happened, or she would have returned within the time window she'd set. But how did he expect to find her? This kind of hopeful optimism wasn't something he did anymore, so why try now when he knew full well that the odds weren't great?

He wasn't the kind of guy who liked to sit and wait except when it was necessary, and right now it was the opposite. He needed to be doing something, both for himself but also, he suspected, for Jordyn.

For the second time today, he'd wished he still prayed. He could, he supposed, and he knew God would listen. It was funny how no matter how far he wandered from what he'd once believed, he didn't question the Truth of all the things he'd learned as a kid. He just didn't know if he wanted to open that door up again. It wasn't that he blamed God for Tori's death; he didn't. A person had killed Tori. He had seen enough to know that people could be awful, evil, and he believed God had given people choices.

It was more that…he'd been so sure that God was going to lead them to Tori. Alive. He'd been convinced, full of faith, and had stayed close to the investigation so that he'd have a front-row seat to what he'd anticipated at the time was a foregone conclusion, the miracle of her being found, unscathed. Instead, he'd watched the investigation slow, then languish, then stop altogether. The case was cold now, officially. Why had he had so much faith if it was all just going to come to nothing? If God wasn't going to have them find her alive? Or, for that matter, at all? All that hoping had left him sick, feeling…

Well, hurt. Why let him hope only to be silent? God *could* have helped them find her, if only for closure. And yet, they were always going to have to wonder and live with the knowledge that whoever had ended Tori's life walked free, their life entirely unaffected.

Even now, years later, it was too painful to keep considering. It drove him, during his workdays, to dig deeper, to find answers. Answers were something it was easy to take for granted until you had none. Finn would never take answers for granted again.

Though as he followed Cipher deeper into the woods, he hoped she could find answers.

Finn wasn't sure enough about how search dogs worked to know if she would be able to find a person, even if it was Jordyn, without Jordyn there.

If she was close, the dog would change how she acted, right?

That was what brought them this far, after all.

When so much time had passed with no sign of Jordyn, he'd watched for her on the main road, where she'd be coming from town toward the west. When she didn't appear, it occurred to him: it was entirely possible that she'd disappeared on the way *to* town, not from town, which meant he didn't want to search too far away. But he was on foot, with no transportation.

And only Cipher as a guide.

According to his watch, he'd been walking with the K-9 for about ten minutes when she'd veered off the main trail and into the woods. Her behavior seemed similar to how it had been earlier, when she'd found the blood on the trail. There were different alerts for living and dead people, he remembered Jordyn telling him that earlier in the day, but he didn't remember what the difference was, and a pit opened in his stomach. He hadn't really let himself consider that he might be too late finding Jordyn. In his mind, if he left the house, he'd find her.

Maybe he had more blind optimism remaining than he'd realized.

As he followed Cipher, doing his best on the uneven terrain, dodging tree branches as he squeezed through gaps that the dog easily fit through, he found himself hoping she would be okay. He wasn't willing to let himself entertain the possibly that she might not be, despite the pit in his stomach.

Cipher picked up her pace even more, and he did the same, until they were standing in the middle of the forest. He looked around but saw nothing. Cipher ran to a cluster of downed spruce trees and sat then yipped.

This wasn't the same signal from the other day. This was different. He felt himself take a deep breath, dare a little more to hope, as he moved closer. Ridiculous as he felt talking to spruce trees—as he saw absolutely nothing to indicate that Jordyn was here—he called her name anyway, softly.

"Jordyn?"

"Finn? Cipher? What are you doing?" she called back. Gratitude surged in his chest.

"Looking for you."

"You don't...why would you..." The branches rustled. "Did you see anyone?"

"No one."

"And no one saw you?"

"Not that I know of. Are you okay?" He was out of breath, both from following behind Cipher while his head pounded and also from...worry?

Not that he wasn't used to worrying about people. He was. But the level of relief he'd felt when he saw Jordyn went past that. He didn't want any harm to come to her.

While he'd known that, at least on a conceptual level, he hadn't realized how deeply he cared.

She pushed herself through the branches and marveled at how well camouflaged she'd been. "Not now," she said. "We'll talk at my house. Which way did you come from? Let's go back the same way."

She'd been on the ground and stayed crouched down to pet Cipher behind the ears. The dog looked proud of herself, and Finn was proud of her too. What had felt like a complete shot in the dark to him had been business as usual for the search and rescue dog. He'd never realized how dependable they were.

"This way," he told Jordyn, motioning to the path Cipher had taken that would lead them back to the main trail. Moving at almost a run, they made it back to Jordyn's house in no time.

Her place was in a little clearing in a thickly wooded area, even though it was technically in a neighborhood. It was a really Alaskan neighborhood, he'd seen yesterday on the drive in. Spread out houses, several acres of land with each one, catering to that feeling of independence it seemed Alaskans cherished so much. He felt himself breathe a massive sigh of relief when they were all back inside.

Unseen. At least, he was pretty sure.

But that didn't mean the threat was gone. Whoever was after her wasn't likely to give up or assume Finn dead already without seeing a body. And if Jordyn had been hiding in the woods, then his instinct had been right and something had happened tonight.

He tried to respect the time she seemed to need to process as Jordyn went through the motions of feeding Cipher a snack and giving her a toy, presumably as a treat for finding her. Then she made coffee. She poured it into two mugs, stopping halfway through pouring the second to look up at Finn.

"I didn't even think to ask if you wanted coffee, just assumed."

"You assumed right."

"Cream? Sugar?"

"Both," he said, and she raised her eyebrows. Finn laughed at the expression on her face. "What?"

"Somehow I pegged you for one of those guys who drinks it black. You know, serious coffee."

"Oh, I'm serious about coffee. I'm just also serious about sugar, and the cream makes it better." He shrugged. "I can make it, though."

She waved him off. "I've got it."

He watched her while she worked, noticing how competent she was, how the calm she seemed to possess was almost contagious. He knew something was wrong. But watching her make coffee, he didn't feel like they were avoiding the hard conversation. It felt like he could just… wait. Trust that things might be okay. She inspired that kind of confidence, just being around her.

It was attractive. *She* was attractive. The realization hit him, and he blinked away. He appreciated what she'd done for him, had been impressed by the way she'd worked that morning…why the sudden attraction to her now, in her kitchen, watching her make coffee? Was it just the shock earlier of the danger she was in, some kind of feeling of obligation to keep her safe? Finn shoved the thoughts back, like he'd tried to do with varying levels of success when they were teenagers. If ever there were a bad time for starting a romance, it was now. They were both in too much danger for any kind of distraction. Besides, he was leav-

ing the state. It wouldn't be fair to either of them, even if
she *were* interested, which she wasn't. As far as he knew.

"Here you go." She handed him the coffee, her movements still relaxed, so much so that he felt his own shoulders relaxing.

They walked into the living room. He sat down on the
couch, and she sat beside him, angling herself to face him.
"We have a problem," she finally said after taking a sip or
two of coffee while Finn waited.

"We have more than one problem. But tell me about
this one."

"Someone definitely thinks I know something," she said,
and Finn felt his stomach drop. It wasn't random, then, whatever had happened. Even though the break-in could have
been targeted at Jordyn, if the killer had seen her find Finn
and wanted to track down information on his whereabouts—
and he'd continued to lie low in case it was and the killer
didn't know he was definitely still alive—this confirmed
that Jordyn was in danger, with or without him here. She
was now a target. Of a serial killer who wouldn't hesitate
to kill again.

# EIGHT

Finn's face had gone completely unreadable once she said someone was after her. It was something in the way his jaw seemed to relax, clearly artificially, like he was making an effort not to give away how tense the news actually made him. His brown eyes darkened, only a hint, but enough that she saw it. She'd been studying him so closely since she'd found him the other night, looking for signs his condition might have changed or that he needed to be seen by a doctor, and the attention had resulted in an unexpected familiarity with his face and facial expressions.

He had a nice face, she'd realized. Handsome. More handsome than she'd ever let herself admit.

She shoved the thoughts away, like she'd done so often when she was younger.

"Everything was fine at the police department. I talked to my sergeant, let him know about the blood, and for the most part managed to avoid talking to any law enforcement besides Sergeant Patrick, who I'm pretty sure I can trust. Melissa and Officer Lee did both catch me on the way out. I'm sure some of the others knew I'd been in there, though, as the admin did make a big deal of seeing me."

"Like she wanted someone else to hear?"

She shook her head. "No, I think she was just genu-inely glad."

"Did anyone mention me?"

"My boss, yeah. He wanted to know if I knew you, if we were close, all of that."

"And what did you say?"

"That we barely knew each other as kids, and that we lost touch after you moved." She looked up at him, trying again to gauge his expression. Could she read it well enough yet to see if that news affected him at all?

No, his face gave away none of his secrets, at least not to her. But she couldn't help but wonder if that truth affected him the way it did her. They'd both been so determined to not break that unspoken rule, where little sisters' best friends were off-limits, as were best friends' older broth-ers. Then, when Tori disappeared, there was no founda-tion of friendship. In their shock and grief, they'd lashed out at each other. But imagine the ways they could have been there for each other, encouraged each other, after Tori's death, if they'd tried being friends. They couldn't get back that time.

"Did he give you any details of what they think hap-pened to me?" Finn asked.

It was a strange question, and she smiled a little at the unusualness of this entire situation. "I tried to find out—subtly, before you even ask—but it doesn't sound like they've developed much of an opinion yet. Maybe you're a person of interest, maybe you're a victim...they just know you've disappeared."

Finn nodded. "What happened after you left the police department?"

"I was distracted, which is stupid. I should have known better."

"Hey." He reached a hand out to cover hers, and they made contact for maybe half a second before he pulled his hand away. Jordyn blinked, half wondering if she'd imagined his touch, but no, her hand still felt warm where his had been. She shook her head. Hadn't she already learned that getting distracted in this situation would do her no good at all?

"It wasn't your fault." He kept talking. "Whatever happened, it definitely wasn't your fault. You aren't supposed to be in situations like this, right? As a search and rescue worker?"

She considered that, tipped her head to the side a bit. "I mean, no. But we are supposed to be more aware of our surroundings than I was today, that's for sure. I just had so much on my mind. Whatever you say, it was stupid. I knew better."

He sighed. "I'm sorry you're in this position at all. It's because of me."

She wasn't going to try to argue with that because it wasn't like he was wrong. If Cipher hadn't found him lying on the ground, she'd probably still be out there searching for bodies, on the edges of danger instead of in the thick of it. But where would that leave him?

She was afraid she knew the answer. Surely whoever had harmed him had anticipated that he'd die there of his injuries and would have returned later to check or finish the job.

"The killer was moving the body then coming back for you, weren't they?" she said aloud, knowing it was conversational whiplash, but unable to abandon the thought now that she'd had it. "That's got to be what happened."

"Likely."

"You'd already thought of that, hadn't you?" she said. She should've known he'd be one step ahead of her. But that was extremely encouraging, from a medical standpoint. His reasoning skills didn't seem to be at all affected by his injury anymore, if they ever had been. That was a good sign.

She needed to share the rest of what had happened. "I noticed the car following me a handful of miles outside of town. It was too late to do much, though I did try to vary my speed to see if they were really committed to following me, and they were. They ran me off the road just after the bridge into my neighborhood then started chasing me on foot. I ran."

"Who?" His tone was casual but urgent. Like he desperately wanted the answer to this question, to fill the gap in his memory and bring them closer to the end of this madness, but like he didn't want to pressure her.

"I don't know." She hated the truth as much as he did in that moment, she was sure. "But I couldn't tell. They had a hat pulled down low over their face, I could tell that much from my rearview mirror."

He nodded.

"When they were chasing me, it was through muskeg swamp, and I had to focus on my feet. I glanced back once, I think. Maybe twice. But I never saw anything besides movement when I confirmed they were still chasing me."

He nodded, seeming to consider the situation. They hadn't made much more progress, Jordyn knew that. It had to sting him, at least a little. But on the other hand, twenty-four hours ago, he hadn't even been attacked yet, or just had been. It was still before noon. They just hadn't had much time.

"We'll figure it out." His voice was confident. It made her feel better, somehow. Something Jordyn didn't want to read into right now.

She blew out a breath. "Yeah, I know, but I want to figure

it out now." She was able to crack a small smile at herself, hearing her own impatience. Less than twenty-four hours. She needed to remember that.

They were quiet for a few minutes, each sipping their coffee. Then Finn nudged her arm gently. "Hey."

She looked at him, aware of how close they'd ended up on the couch. "Yeah?"

"I realized something when I was waiting for you and pacing your house."

"What's that?" She sat up a little straighter, hoping it was something that would help with this case.

"It wasn't information, really, I was just realizing we never really talked. About Tori and all of that."

Her mood sank.

Tori. It seemed impossible that someone who always had a smile on her face, the quintessential homecoming queen type that was well liked by everyone, could be dead. People like that just seemed immortal somehow, but everyone had their breaking point. Every human life was delicate and fragile.

She nodded. "Yeah. We didn't."

"I'm sorry for how that all happened. That's part of what I wanted to say to you."

She frowned. "It wasn't your fault, Finn."

"That's not what I meant, I meant the way you and I argued during the investigation. I already saw earlier today when Cipher was helping you find things in that clearing that I sold search dogs short. And decided that I wanted to apologize. I was a jerk during that search, and I'm sorry."

"You'd lost your sister."

"And you'd lost your best friend."

The discordant silence, the hum of loss that was almost palpable between them, was exactly what Jordyn had thought, only a few minutes before, that they'd missed out on because of their refusal to have any kind of relationship, even a friendship, with each other. This felt redemptive somehow, like it made up for that.

"I wasn't exactly gracious about your insistence that the search dogs were a waste of time," she admitted. "So I'm sorry too."

"Start over?"

"There's nothing to start over," she told him, sadly. "All of that's over." Except it wasn't, was it? For Jordyn, maybe it would never seem over. It wasn't like you could get over a loss like that. But more than the invisible idea of grief and the way it tended to haunt you, it was never going to seem over without her body being found and given a proper burial. This unfinished-ness would always make it feel like it wasn't over. Not really.

Finn must have been able to read the well-intentioned lie on her face. "I don't think so," he said softly. Then he continued. "Is she why?"

"Is she why what?"

"Why you got into search and rescue work?"

It probably wasn't too hard to guess, but Jordyn still felt a little too seen, like he'd walked in and started to read her better than anyone ever could. Her personal life being nonexistent was mostly her fault. She held herself at arm's length from people now, never let anyone close. She'd tried to date, had even had a few relationships pass the one month mark, but they always ended the same when the men expressed their disappointment that it seemed like no matter how hard they tried, they didn't really know her at all.

Only one of them had meant it in an inappropriate way, and she had very definitely told him where he could stick that idea. The others? She hadn't defended herself against those words at all. Because they were right. It was true.

"Yeah," she admitted to him now because why not? He seemed to know already. "She's why."

"Me too," he admitted, and Jordyn thought his voice sounded vulnerable, like maybe this wasn't something he was used to talking about either. "It sounds ridiculous, right? It's not like being in the FBI was going to bring her back, but..."

"But you could stop it for someone else," she offered.

"Exactly."

A long few minutes passed, and the silence ebbed between them gently, like the lazy flow of a river, not at all like the awkward, stretched-out kind of silence Jordyn had experienced before with other people.

She cleared her throat. "I should go look at search grids, try to figure out where I should go next. I haven't officially heard where I'm assigned to search next, but I'm expecting I'll hear from Sergeant Patrick later today or maybe in the morning."

"You're not really going back out there."

"Absolutely." She didn't know how true it was until she said it, but Jordyn felt the word with every fiber of her being. Maybe it would be expected if her experience earlier, being run off the road, running for her life, had scared her away from the search. After all, this morning, even Sergeant Patrick had questioned whether it was safe to have search and rescue workers out since an FBI agent had disappeared. She'd pushed back then, but that was without any proof that this had turned personal, that someone was after *her* in general. Now that she had that proof, she felt provoked. Determined.

If someone wanted a fight, she was going to give them

one. If she'd felt like she could walk away earlier, she definitely did not feel that way anymore.

Bringing her into this by making her a target was something this killer would live to regret.

Flashes of memories came to her then. The blood in the grass. The last victim of this serial killer that Cipher had found, tucked beside some rocks next to a creek.

The situation was dangerous, and the killer was not to be underestimated. She knew this even better than most. But still...

They'd made it personal. And Jordyn wasn't one to back down.

Finn had been staring at her, maybe trying to read something in her face.

"It's not safe," he said, his own face serious.

"I didn't say it was. But I need to do it."

She thought he would try to talk her out of it in some way, or tell her all the reasons it was a terrible idea, but after a few more seconds, he only nodded. "I'm coming too, then."

"Someone will see you." It would never work. There were no scenarios where it would. She knew, because she'd already thought of it. There were sometimes situations where search and rescue workers would be paired with someone else who wasn't SAR on a search, for safety, sometimes law enforcement, but at the moment there weren't many people Jordyn wanted to be alone in the woods with. The list was near zero. She'd feel fine with Finn out there, though, and she'd already wished he could go with her and Cipher. But his safety was important too, and the chances of someone realizing he was out there and going after him were too high.

"It may be worth it." He seemed to be considering all

the angles too. At least she had some degree of assurance he wasn't rushing into this. "Let me know when you hear from your boss about the grid and the plan?"

She nodded. "He'll want to get a team up to look at that blood today, and that'll be his focus, not the active search for her body, I think. Because something they find at the scene today could inform where we'd go next. If they're able to find some evidence today it could turn the search into something more achievable than finding a needle in a haystack."

"That's a solid point. Keep me posted?"

"Yeah, I will."

The rest of the day passed uneventfully. Jordyn studied maps of the area where she'd been searching yesterday and today, got a feel for the trails and topography of the surrounding areas where she might be sent. Some of it she'd hiked before and was at least marginally familiar with, but some of the areas near where they'd been today were swampy. It wasn't very close to her house, but the topography was similar. Then another nearby place had a deep ravine with a stream at the bottom of it. The Kenai Peninsula was a region of variety as far as land, and the search area was a good representation of that.

They ate dinner—macaroni and cheese, homemade at least, but she really needed to get to the store soon—and then they sat around. Jordyn wanted to tell Finn to take a break, that he should be on some level of brain rest after what was almost certainly a concussion, but he'd spent the entire afternoon on the couch with a notebook, scribbling away. It looked to her like he was trying to get every thought related to the case out of his brain and on paper. She wasn't sure it was a bad idea either, but it looked exhausting.

"Want to talk about it?" she'd asked him at one point, but he'd shaken his head.

Whatever weird closeness she may have started to feel with him earlier had mostly evaporated now as Finn had seemed to turn inside himself. At least it made sense. They'd talked about Tori, talked about how that was part of their motivation...it seemed even just discussing it had made Finn lock in and put his sole focus on sorting out what he knew about the case and what he still needed to know.

Or...or was it her almost being hurt today?

Even if it was, it wasn't personal. It wasn't like her being in danger hit him harder than someone else. At least probably not. They'd barely known each other before, and they sure didn't know each other now.

As she worked on straightening up a few things in the house—part of her bedtime routine—she glanced over her shoulder now and then to where he was working. She couldn't say she was unattracted to him on a normal day, but now when his eyebrows were pressed together in concentration, the way he was chewing on the end of a pencil without seeming to notice, all because he was working on the puzzle that was this case...it was hard to ignore.

She should get out more, maybe. Date. Because surely any kind of attraction she had to him was just some leftover teenage rebellion sort of crush, right? It was a sign she needed to really try to move on.

With her mind going in too many directions, Jordyn finally double-checked all the doors as Cipher walked the circuit of the inside of the house with her, giving no evidence of alarm.

"I'm going to go to sleep," she called to him.

"Mmm" was all Finn said.

"You're okay in the guest cabin?" It was more of a guest

suite, really, as it connected to the main house, but it had its own door, so they'd be in separate quarters. Great for privacy, bad if someone broke in in the middle of the night to attack either one of them. At least she'd have Cipher.

"Yeah, I'm fine," he said, barely looking up from the paper.

Jordyn was far from tired, but she knew if she was going to stay aware enough to contribute to the search she needed to get some rest. That and being in the same room as Finn was...

He was so much more than just Tori's brother, and somehow that was how she'd always seen him. That was the label that floated, invisible, above his head every time she interacted with him. And that was still how she thought of him; it wasn't as though that connection would ever disappear, but...

He was becoming more than her friend's brother now. And there were too many other things going on in her mind for her to process it at the moment.

So instead she left, fully aware that she was avoiding a situation that might feel better tomorrow, or might still require her to dig deep and confront the shifting dynamics of their relationship.

But for tonight, she could sleep. If she could forget about the fact that someone out there wanted her dead.

# NINE

Finn hadn't wanted to sleep. He'd been too busy thinking, trying to remember, documenting every detail that came to mind about the current case, but he'd felt himself nodding off sometime around one in the morning and decided it would be better to go get some sleep than to risk being off his game the next day.

He'd set an alarm for four, giving himself only a few hours of sleep, but it was enough. He'd awaken without a headache—the first time he hadn't had one since this started...had it only been two days ago? Day before yesterday, Jordyn and Cipher had found him. The lack of headache seemed like a good sign. He didn't dare let himself hope that his memory had returned, not really, but a tiny part of him must have still entertained the idea because when he tried to think back on what had led to him being apparently left for dead on the Alaskan ground, he still came up empty.

Frustration tightened his chest and throat, and Finn wished he had freedom of movement to go for a run or something, but first of all it would be foolish to risk going out where people could see him when it was for no good reason at all, and second he wasn't going to leave Jordyn alone.

Instead, even though it was early, he headed into the main house through the connecting door. Coffee might help his brain wake up enough to be of some use to him. He was waiting for it, starting to hear the familiar sizzle, when he heard a creaking sound behind him and whirled around, his entire being on alert.

Jordyn stood on the stairs with her hands raised in a mock surrender pose and laughed. "Don't shoot?"

The joke fell a little flat as Finn thought about all the things that had happened to them both over the last forty-eight hours. Joking about getting shot wasn't really funny. He did understand her desire to lighten the mood, though.

Whatever had passed between them last night had had her running out of the room at the first moment. Those minutes they'd talked about Tori and their own careers had been one of the strangest conversations he'd ever had. Strange, because he hadn't felt like he needed to guard what he said. She didn't seem like she had either, and they'd both been honest to the point of vulnerable. After the conversation, before she'd left the room, from her perspective, he'd probably seemed focused on what he was doing, he guessed, but the truth was that he'd noticed the shift between them too and wasn't sure what to do about it. With that in mind he'd just sort of buried himself in the case and tried not to think about it. Avoidance might not be the healthiest coping strategy, but it was one he'd employed well over the years.

"Couldn't sleep?" he asked her, as he pulled mugs from the cabinet and poured them each a cup of the hot coffee.

She took it from him when he offered it to her. "Not well." Her voice was flat. "Yesterday bothered me more than I thought it did."

"Having someone after you?"

"Yes. It was incredibly personal. The feeling of being

intentionally pursued through the woods…" She trailed off, took a sip of her drink and then looked away from him. "I dreamed about Tori. And what she must have felt, and…" Her voice wavered, and she took another sip then set the mug down on the counter and rubbed her forehead with one hand like she was trying to ease a tension headache.

"Hey." He put his hand on her upper arm, just a light touch meant to reassure her. "You're okay though."

"But I might not have been. Tori wasn't. The girl, Nicole Collins, who we were looking for wasn't. Why them and not me? How likely is it that I'll be next? It's all the same."

She was well and truly crying now, and Finn didn't know how to process it. Tears were streaming boldly down her cheeks. He should have known that Jordyn Williams was not the type to cry apologetically or hesitantly. Her protective shell was so thick, but when it was gone, she was so genuinely herself all the time, feeling her feelings fully and inviting you into them. He'd forgotten that, but he'd seen glimpses of it when she'd been best friends with his sister.

His sister. What Jordyn had said just now…

"It's all the same," he said aloud, repeating her words. She looked at him, confusion mixing with the tears in her eyes. "It's all the same," he said again.

Jordyn frowned. "I mean, it's not, you know. But it is. It felt like it. I felt like they must have felt."

He paused, stopping in his tracks physically though his mind was still whirring. Whatever this revelation was, it could wait. Jordyn couldn't. "I hate that you felt that way."

Could he hug her? He reached his arms out, waited.

She stepped into them, and he wrapped his arms around her back and held her tight. He thought he felt her breathing steady, away from the shuddering breaths, and then released her from his hold.

Neither of them moved. They just stared at each other.

Jordyn broke the silence. "Now what is the same? What were you saying?"

"I'm not sure, it's just…" He blinked. Tried to make sense of his racing thoughts. He felt Jordyn standing close still, waiting, but he needed to be able to explain clearly. Too many things about investigating this serial killer case had reminded him of Tori's unsolved cold case. But he'd assumed they were separate. Why wouldn't he have? It wasn't as though murder was commonplace in Alaska, but it certainly wasn't rare. And women disappearing? The state, beautiful though it was, had a serious problem with that. These incidents didn't feel unique enough for him to find any kind of tie between his sister's disappearance and presumed death years ago and the current serial killer case.

Except, weren't they?

A woman had been killed. Her body was hidden somewhere in the wilderness.

The only real difference was that Tori had never been found. And all the others had, hadn't they?

He could visualize the spot where they'd been yesterday, the quiet area that should have been peaceful but was wrecked by evil, and it had felt haunting instead. The wilderness could hold very tightly to its secrets. Was it possible Tori wasn't the only one killed years ago? Or was she truly the only one, some kind of practice?

As he ran all the scenarios in his mind, one fact kept coming back up.

He was pretty sure Tori's killer and this killer were one and the same.

And suddenly, he was also pretty sure that before he'd been attacked, he'd had at least some proof of this. Or suspicions. More than the tangle of thoughts he had now.

"Finn? You okay?"

He looked back at Jordyn, having forgotten she was there for a minute. He couldn't help the grin that spread across his face. Not because the subject was cheery. On the contrary, it was heavy and overwhelming, and sometimes he didn't know how he could possibly be expected to carry around this kind of burden while simultaneously acting like everything was okay. But he smiled because he finally felt some level of forward movement.

"I remembered something."

And quickly the woman who had beautifully expressed her heartbroken sadness without any level of shame or holding back wiped her eyes and seemed to be waiting for what he'd have to say. "Yeah?"

"It's all the same. Like you said."

She raised her eyebrows but said nothing as she waited for him to explain.

"I think the same person who killed my sister is killing these women too. It feels familiar, and I don't think it's just because the past is stuck in our heads."

A shiver ran down his arms as he said the words aloud, and it felt like a definite statement when he said it.

If he'd wondered how she'd respond, he shouldn't have. Within seconds, she was on the phone to the police department, asking for all their records of the Tori McDaniel case.

Their coffee lukewarm, Finn and Jordyn moved to the living room to drink it and started to comb through old case files that Sergeant Patrick must have emailed them over immediately.

It wasn't much, Finn knew. Still a needle in the proverbial haystack, but at least they'd just gotten more specific in what they were looking for, and it was possible that there might be some way to broaden the search using information from when his sister had disappeared.

The file on Tori wasn't as thick as he'd like it to be, but as he read through it, he did so slowly, as though he'd not seen any of the details, desperate to somehow find something in this reading that would give him some kind of a hint as to who was behind it.

Tori McDaniel. Twenty. Missing female from Eagle Bend, Alaska.

It was clinical. And it was his sister. He blinked away moisture from his eyes as he took a long sip of coffee, processing the rest in his mind like a story.

She'd disappeared in the evening after work, and Tori's parents had reported her missing to police at nine the next morning, when she still hadn't come home. They hadn't wanted to jump the gun. Their adult daughter not being home was cause for alarm, but not to the degree that they'd thought it was necessary to get the police involved.

Police started to search near the coffee shop. Tori's car wasn't in the lot. The search continued into the heart of Eagle Bend. Then, on the third day of the search, when more details were released to the public in the hopes of generating some kind of information, an anonymous caller had reported seeing someone matching Tori's description hiking a remote trail in the opposite direction of town, up in the more mountainous area on the north side of Eagle Bend. She'd been seen by someone else picking her way across a tricky boulder field at the base of a mountain.

The search had intensified. Hopes would be raised by a discovery—a bit of Tori's jacket had been found caught on a tree. And they'd seen footprints, only to investigate further and realize they belonged to a woman who was much taller than Tori—who'd been frequently teased by Finn for her five-foot-two height in a family that was known for being tall—and were unconnected to the case. The small town had been uneasy, having lost one of their own unexpectedly. Anxiety around town escalated when another woman, Jenna Matthews, had disappeared. But she'd turned up hours after her family had made the police report to the Eagle Bend Police Department, alive and unharmed and with a satisfactory explanation as to where she'd been. Apparently she'd gotten lost hiking, and police started to think something similar may have happened to Tori and that foul play may not have been a factor after all. In his gut, though, Finn had always known that his sister knew Alaska too well to have disappeared. She would never have underestimated the backcountry the way some people did. Someone had killed her. But he had no proof.

After that, the trail to find Tori had gone colder than a January day in the mountains. Eventually it had been shelved. Officially labeled a cold case.

And yet…for the first time in the forty-eight hours since he'd lost his short-term memory, Finn felt real hope for this case. He knew there was something tying these two investigations together—they just needed to find it. Stopping this killer could bring Tori justice.

As he glanced over at Jordyn, he thought he honestly might see a little hope for his life in general.

He would just have to wait and see.

It was just past nine when Jordyn's hunger wouldn't let her work anymore. She sat up straight; she'd been hunching over case files since about seven this morning.

Had it really only been two hours? She felt like she'd lived and relived lifetimes as she'd read back through the old case files. It was easier to read than it had been to live through, since she could try to distance herself from it slightly without the emotional impact it had had at the time. She knew now that there was no happy ending. Tori hadn't been found. Somehow the distance made that easier.

But also harder. Because losing your best friend should never get "easier."

"You hungry?" she asked Finn, and he looked at her like she'd entirely lost her coherent mind.

"I don't usually eat while I work."

"Really?" Jordyn raised her eyebrows as she stood and walked toward the kitchen. "I always eat while I work."

In half an hour, she'd cooked blueberry scones with some blueberries she'd found in the freezer from last berry season and some bacon. Cipher had had a bite or two of bacon, and Finn had even come wandering into the kitchen.

"I mean, if you're cooking…" he said with a smile.

She waited till he finished eating to tell him what she'd realized right before she'd gotten up to cook.

"We have to go back," she finally said.

"Back to where?"

She pointed to the map, waited for him to say something.

"Tori's point last seen." His voice was flat and expressionless, and she looked at him, not sure what she was expecting to see. How was this for him, to relive what had to be the worst experience of his life?

She should go alone, leave him here. Only she and Cipher really needed to be there, though his law enforcement perspective would be appreciated.

"If the cases are connected, then what we are looking for now may be something we find by looking backward."

His eyes met hers then, and she saw something of a spark in them. "You sure?"

"Yeah."

"So…not starting over after all?" he asked, hesitantly, and Jordyn heard all the things he wasn't saying, at least she thought she did.

"Sounds like," she said slowly, "we're going to need to look back before we can move ahead."

Finn nodded in agreement. "Absolutely."

He was handsome this morning, a beard growing in around his jaw. It was sandy colored, half a shade lighter than his hair, which looked messy from all the times he'd run his hand through it this morning when he was thinking. Nothing about him was polished, though, or predictably handsome. Instead he looked like the handsomeness was an afterthought. An accident or a casual addition.

*He's leaving as soon as this case is over.*

Still, she'd be lying to herself if she said she didn't find him attractive. Not just how he looked, but his work ethic.

If she'd ever allowed herself the luxury of falling for someone, it would have been someone a lot like Finn McDaniel, she realized, looking at him now.

Jordyn blinked and looked away, but the feeling of the eye contact stayed with her. Wouldn't shake out of her brain.

Why? Why him? Why now? What an awful time to realize how easy it would be to have feelings for him.

She cleared her throat and stood, then busied herself with gathering dishes to wash. "Maybe you should stay here?" She asked it as a question, not wanting him to think she was telling him not to go with them, since that seemed like a guaranteed way to get him to go.

"Why?"

"It's got to be hard for you."

"Worse than for you?"

"She was your sister. That beats best friend."

"I don't think grief really works like that, with comparisons. Grief is just…grief."

Another silence, and she knew if she let herself look at him, he'd be looking back at her with understanding in his eyes.

She wasn't sure she could handle being understood right now, wasn't certain she could withstand how vulnerable it would make her feel. And was entirely certain it would be one more push of her heart in his direction.

"Maybe you're right," she said without meeting his gaze as she continued to clean up after breakfast. The only problem was that Finn had moved to the sink to help her and was washing the dishes she'd been collecting, leaving her with the option to either walk away, which seemed rude, or to dry the dishes after he'd rinsed them.

She chose that one, standing beside him, aware of how close he was to her, not looking at him.

"So yeah, I'm going," he finally said, and when she glanced up at him, he looked away.

Maybe she wasn't the only one trying to figure out what on earth was going on here.

After the cleanup, they went their separate ways to prep for the day. Jordyn got her and Cipher's gear ready, putting Cipher's vest on her before they even got into the car so she'd know they were going to work. Jordyn wasn't harboring any hope they'd find Tori's body *this* time, as though her and Finn searching together would somehow unveil something no one had been able to discover for years. It was more that she wanted Cipher to be paying attention, in case there was anything else. Bodies, live humans…anything strange on this trail that Jordyn and Finn's human senses could miss, Jordyn wanted to know about.

"Will anyone from the search be near this area?" he asked her as they drove down the road, and she shook her head.

"No, while the areas would connect eventually, like there are trails between the two, they're two separate areas, where Tori was last seen and where the current search is." That was one thing in their favor, at least, that no one from the current investigation should see them. She still wasn't entirely certain it was safe for Finn to be out, but she was learning that Finn prioritized his own safety somewhere very close to last on his list of goals.

Not that he'd been risky—she wouldn't say that from the brief time they'd been back in each other's lives. She just could tell that he held his life loosely. Like he wanted to make it count, but he was the kind of man who would rather be out righting wrongs, even if it was more dangerous than hiding at home making sure he'd live as many years as possible.

They were both quiet on the drive to the pullout where Tori had been seen last by another hiker who'd taken this more isolated route. It was a trailhead, but only a small one off the side of the road with room for four or so cars.

"Ready?" she asked when they pulled in. Finn looked distracted but answered in the affirmative.

He could afford to be distracted, she supposed. It wasn't as though she was counting on him on this search, though another set of eyes would be nice. Frankly, if no one had found anything relating to Tori's disappearance years ago, she highly doubted there was anything to be found. But searching the area seemed wise in light of Finn's realization that his sister's killer might be this same one.

Somehow the full force of that hadn't hit her till just now, but she felt the chills run up her spine at the thought. What had happened to Finn, the raw violence of it, was shocking enough already without adding to it. Knowing it might have been the same person? Jordyn couldn't even process how that would feel, to know for sure that was true.

Maybe it was foolish to come here, as though retracing Tori's steps would give them any new leads so many years after her disappearance. But it was the only idea she'd had.

"I haven't been here in forever," she said aloud, mostly to herself, but Finn turned and looked at her.

"You've been back? Since the search?"

"Yeah." She nodded. It had scared her the first few times, led to some nightmares about the same thing happening to her, but when the search had been officially closed, she hadn't felt like everything possible had been done. So as soon as she'd learned how to handle search dogs and gotten Cipher, she'd spent a bit of time here, wandering around, trying to find…something. Anything.

The wilderness gave up absolutely no hints.

Was it possible today could be different?

"Oh," Finn said, nodding.

Jordyn didn't really want to talk about it, but somehow Finn's lack of comment drove her to say something. "What? What do you mean 'oh'?"

"I just didn't know you came up here. Alone?"

They'd been walking across the parking lot and finally made their way onto the start of the trail. A shiver ran down her spine. The one problem with being here was that it put her in Tori's shoes in a way that was entirely uncomfortable and eerie.

"Well, yeah. No one else wanted to hike up here after that, and besides, who would I have gone with?" It wasn't like she'd had a whole group of friends. She and Tori had friends besides each other in high school, but when Jordyn went away to college, she hadn't really kept up with most of her friends back home, thinking she was beyond that now, not returning. Definitely not permanently.

When she couldn't bring herself to go back to her psychology degree at the University of Washington and had moved home, she'd rearranged her life in a way she still didn't know how to quantify.

"You could have called me," he said.

"You were busy. Hurting."

"So were you."

"And as we've already talked about, we weren't friends."

"Why was that, again?"

Her eyes widened. "Uh…" How did she even answer that question without sounding presumptuous? Telling him she hadn't been friends with him because she figured dating her friend's older brother was off-limits sounded way too honest. It assumed that if they'd been friends they also would have eventually dated. But that was the only reason she had. She'd been kind of sad they weren't friends back then, even at the time. He'd seemed like a cool person. Athletic, funny, but not one of those guys who was full of himself.

"Come on, we're adults, let's just talk about it. I'll start. I thought you were amazing. But before you moved to town, a friend of my sister's had a crush on me, and when our middle school relationship predictably didn't lead to happily-ever-after, she stopped being friends with Tori, hurt her pretty badly. I decided after that it was better if I just stayed away from all of Tori's friends, so I wouldn't risk that happening again. And then you moved to town, and as interesting and cool as you were, I knew it would be entirely too easy to like you as more than a friend. So that's why I kept my distance…how about you?"

Several sentences ago, Jordyn had stopped walking. She

blinked a few times, working to process what he'd said and what he hadn't said.

"I, uh…" She cleared her throat. "Yeah. I definitely got a 'my brother is off-limits' vibe. Makes sense there was a whole story behind it."

He nodded, waiting for her to answer his question. Something she had no intention of doing. She just…couldn't, right now.

His stare was intense, and he wasn't backing down. She took a deep breath, tried to think, but found it almost impossible with him staring at her like this.

It was just because her emotions were raw, wasn't it? She'd tried, so many times over the past five years, to start a meaningful relationship with someone. It wasn't that she'd dated everyone on the planet, but she'd tried everything she could think of. Blind dates. Dating apps. Nothing ever lasted more than a couple of dates, and inevitably, men thought she was the problem. She wouldn't let them get close. They had no idea who she was.

They were right, she knew.

How was it possible that Finn had gotten past her walls so quickly, and without her even trying to start any kind of relationship?

He saw her.

And it scared her almost as much as knowing a killer was after her, but for entirely different reasons.

Finally, Finn smiled at her and looked away. Dropping the topic. One more reason to like him. Which meant she'd have to keep working to convince her heart to keep its distance.

# TEN

Unlike the trail that he'd been found on the other day, this one had much more variability in the elevation. It was a dramatic area that ranged topographically from a creek bed to cliffs above it to a boulder field even higher that was likely the remains of an old glacier, tucked into a valley between two mountains. The places to hide a body were numerous, as were the places to slip and have a fatal accident. That was why for the first few days that Tori had been gone, he'd held out hope that maybe she'd disappeared a little more innocuously. Slipped in the boulder field, had an accident along the creek. It wasn't that he wished her hurt by accident, but if someone hadn't been after her, if it hadn't been a malicious disappearance, then maybe it was more likely they'd find her unharmed.

That hadn't been the case. If her disappearance had been an accident, they should have found evidence of her body, or of an animal attack, something. Finn was convinced someone had been involved with his sister's disappearance, and local law enforcement seemed to agree during the ensuing investigation. But no evidence ever materialized. The case went cold.

As they wove down the narrow trail deeper into the woods, the light disappeared through the crowding trees.

They seemed taller here than closer to town, and Finn didn't know if it was just a perspective thing, or if their proximity to the creek made them grow taller. Probably that was the case. It would make sense.

He was detaching, he could feel it, building walls around his emotions. Being here was hard. He couldn't imagine Jordyn coming here alone, but somehow knowing that she had made all kinds of sense. She wasn't the kind of woman to abandon a missing friend, even when it was well past the point when most people would have acknowledged that all hope was lost. It was one of the things he admired about her.

He didn't know what he'd been doing earlier, talking with her like that, initiating another deep conversation that made him feel even closer to her. This was hardly the time or place to start a relationship.

For some reason, the determination he'd once had to stay away from Jordyn, especially where romance was concerned, was wavering to the point that it no longer made sense to him that he'd been avoiding her at all. For a brief second when he'd been talking to her earlier, he'd wondered if he was somehow being disloyal to his sister, but that was unreasonable. Tori was gone. They were still here. And frankly even if Tori had been alive, now that they were all adults, they probably would have revisited the "off-limits" rule.

He wished his sister was here now. Of course then they wouldn't be hiking this trail, searching for…whatever they were looking for.

"What are you hoping to find?" he asked Jordyn as he stepped over another tangle of roots growing on the dirt-covered ground, careful not to lose his footing on the narrow and uneven trail. He supported her plan to come here because he was desperate to do something to make himself useful, but just because he was pretty sure Tori's disappearance had something to do with the disappearances of the other women didn't mean there was something for them to find here.

"I wouldn't argue with finding Tori," Jordyn said, not even looking up at him. Instead she was hiking just like she had last time, following closely behind Cipher, who had her nose sometimes up in the air, sometimes lowered to the ground. "But I'm not counting on that. I figured we'd just look for…anything. If it is the same killer, statistically speaking, isn't it pretty common for them to revisit old locations?"

It was, that was the main reason he'd been upset at the idea of her coming here alone. But he hadn't realized she knew that.

Now she looked at him and apparently read his facial expression because her eyebrows rose. "Didn't know I knew?"

He ignored the question. Sort of. He could feel himself making a face that hopefully let her know that he regretted underestimating her. "If the killer is frequenting this location, Cipher would be able to find something, you think? What all is she looking for?"

"People. Alive or dead. Also, things with people's scent on them."

"Like?"

"Torn pieces of clothing, things they may have dropped. Evidence."

Cipher looked entirely in her element. Her face was curved in what he'd started to think of as a trademark husky grin. Maybe not all huskies made that face, but Cipher seemed to consistently, especially when she was in the woods on the trail of something. Like she knew something they didn't know, and he guessed that she usually did. Right now she trotted at a consistent pace, sniffing, taking everything in.

The dog paused just then, sniffing around the edge of the trail. Finn stayed back as Jordyn approached, knowing that, as the handler, she was the one who knew what she was looking for.

"What is it?" he asked.

"I'm not sure." She looked up and frowned. "What do you think?" She stepped back and he moved in front of her, noticing how close she was standing even as he tried to keep his focus on the case.

It was like reading a story with no words, but one he'd read before. The way the plants were tamped down slightly, in a space about a foot wide, on the edge of the trail, maybe for five feet, give or take.

Like someone had dragged a body to the edge of the trail, laid it down, then continued on.

He looked over at Jordyn. "What did Cipher say?"

She looked over at her dog, who was patiently waiting, sitting beside the spot.

"I wouldn't call it a full alert, but she's giving me the impression that this flattened spot was caused by human remains. Recently, judging by her confident response."

"I think so too." He looked up ahead at the trail that curved deeper into the woods. Then looked behind them. "Let's go back. You can call your boss, tell him you found this impression, have them investigate, but I don't think you should be here."

"Why?"

"It's dangerous."

"It's a murder investigation, that part was kind of assumed."

"I don't want you in danger." He'd said as much to her

before, but he meant the words even more now. Before it was a generic desire to protect someone, keep anyone else from coming to harm in this investigation. Then maybe it was because she'd been Tori's friend, and he didn't want anything bad to happen to her.

Now it was just because he liked Jordyn. He enjoyed being around her, thought she was hilarious and beautiful, and the idea of any harm coming to her was entirely intolerable to him.

He was in much, much deeper than he was ready to admit to himself. Finn cleared his throat, kept talking. "Don't you think it's strange that there's a depression in the ground, for apparently no reason? If someone was dragging a body this way, why would they move it off the trail unless they wanted to make sure someone noticed, lead someone in a certain direction?"

"It doesn't work that way. Cipher is trained to detect scent that lingers. Even what's on the trail is enough for her to notice, she didn't need this."

"Yes, but…" Finn's mind was spinning fast, and he didn't know if he was going overboard in his concern because of his head injury or his complicated and growing feelings for Jordyn. "You're putting yourself at risk. What if this was intentional on the part of the killer? A setup to get us where the killer wants us?"

"Why?"

"Jordyn, I learned years ago that if you try to make sense of a serial killer's actions, you will go crazy. There's something wrong with people when they do something like that. You don't want to understand. Trust me, I don't either."

"I really think it's fine." She started to move forward, and instinctively he reached out, caught her arm.

She turned back to him, eyes shooting sparks, but

stopped short, her expression changing as both of them processed the fact that she'd whirled around almost in his arms. She was so close to him. Maybe six inches away. She was tall enough that their eyes were almost level, and she met his gaze without flinching.

"Please, be careful."

Her eyes were searching his now. The tension between them not something he could deny anymore.

He didn't want Jordyn hurt, not just because she'd been his sister's friend or because he didn't want to see anyone hurt. He didn't want Jordyn hurt because he liked her. Appreciated who she was.

He leaned forward a little, his eyes flicking from her eyes to her lips. Then he waited.

She moved forward too. He made himself stay still, leaving the decision up to her. Was he the only one whose feelings were changing?

For at least twenty seconds, they stayed like that.

And then there was a crashing off to the left.

They broke apart quickly. Finn was alert and ready to do his best to defend Jordyn if there was a threat. Jordyn, he noticed, had immediately looked for Cipher.

She was the one who had caused the noise. Something off in the woods had gotten her attention, maybe? Or did she notice a smell?

"She's found something!" Jordyn called back over her shoulder as she ran off after the dog, and Finn found himself whispering a prayer for protection. He felt uneasy about the discovery they'd made beside the trail, still wasn't sure that it hadn't been intentional. He'd have probably noticed that even without Cipher pointing it out, so if it *was* a trap, had it been put there for someone with a search dog? Or for law enforcement? Was there a specific target?

More questions. No answers. For now, he hurried after Jordyn, heart still racing from almost kissing her, mind demanding that he focus on the present, lest his distraction get them both killed.

Cipher was acting strangely. She'd clearly gotten the scent of something and had taken off, which wasn't entirely unusual, even if the dog did usually prefer to stick a bit closer to her handler. But it was more than that. She seemed anxious. Or maybe just very aware of their surroundings. But whatever it was, it had her behaving in a way that seemed wound up, more tense than usual.

It could mean something.

Of course, dogs could also mirror the emotions of their owners or handlers, and Jordyn wasn't exactly operating from a place of even emotions right now.

She was pretty sure that Finn had almost kissed her just now. Or he'd been waiting for her to kiss him. Either way, it had seemed perfectly logical and reasonable at the time, and she probably would have closed the distance between them if Cipher hadn't run off like she had.

What did that mean? Did it have to mean anything?

Up until now she'd been assuming they could dance around any more difficult conversations and just work on this case, a tenuous partnership that wouldn't last long but was their only choice right now. But that almost kiss… That wouldn't be easy to brush off.

For right now, though, she couldn't think about that anyway. Cipher was her first priority in the wilderness like this, her safety and well-being. In addition to focusing on the case itself and seeing what information they could possibly find while they were out here searching. It was long shot, coming out here, she knew. But if Finn was right and the murderer in this current case was the same one who had killed Tori, then this was the only shot she could possibly think of that might work. If nothing turned up on this search effort, she had nothing. Finn would still be in hiding, she'd go back to searching for the missing woman who was presumed dead and…what? Could they tell someone at the police department that the two cases might be connected, get someone to look into that?

Probably not, not without evidence. Finn was the one who had found some possible connections between the two cases as far as similarities in the type of woman who went missing and the way their bodies were disposed of—or presumably disposed of, in Tori's case. It was all circumstantial and in order for any of it to convince other law enforcement, much less someone in court, they'd need more proof. Besides, Finn was currently missing, as far as local and federal law enforcement was concerned.

Cipher stopped moving. Jordyn had to catch herself to avoid running into her.

The dog lifted her nose slightly, seemed to be looking around with a critical eye.

Everything was as expected—Cipher was sniffing, looking for a scent—but everything was slightly off.

"Is she okay? She seems different," Finn said from behind her.

Jordyn reached down to pet her K-9, feeling for injuries on her legs. Nothing. Her whole body was quivering, though, and her tail, while not tucked between her legs, wasn't up and alert like usual.

"Something is bothering her. I don't know what."

"We should get out of here," Finn said. "She looks uneasy. I feel uneasy. Maybe there's a good reason for it."

She wasn't sure he was wrong, but again she was struck

by the thought that if they didn't find anything today, they were at a dead end. Surely that was worth some risks.

On the other hand, something felt off in the woods to her too. The forest appeared dark and empty, but it didn't feel empty. It felt like…it felt like they weren't alone.

Her senses sharpened as chills ran down her back. "Do you think someone else is out here?" she asked Finn, her voice barely audible, even to her own ears.

He would know what she really meant, which was *do you think the killer is out here?*

"I don't know," he whispered back.

They stood there silent for probably more than a minute. He'd leave now if she was in favor of it, Jordyn knew. But she wasn't willing to back down for no reason.

Cipher started walking.

Jordyn glanced over at Finn, whose face was lined with concern, and followed her dog. She made sure to look around, being extremely careful not to miss anything. Being observant was something she was usually pretty good at, but she willed her senses to heighten even more now. Missing something in this situation could be deadly. So far, she didn't see anything unusual or out of place. Even Cipher's behavior seemed normal now. Did that mean that the threat was gone, if there ever had been one?

It wasn't just a potential murderer they needed to watch out for in these woods. The natural hazards were great. Grizzly bears were especially menacing on this part of the Kenai Peninsula. Was it possible that wildlife had interfered with Cipher's search and made her anxious?

They walked a little farther through the woods, and then Jordyn noticed that it was growing lighter and she could see a gap in the trees up ahead. They were gaining in elevation, and up ahead there was some kind of clearing. Jordyn knew there was a boulder field somewhere in this area because it was a place she'd searched extensively during the initial search for Tori and for some time after. It seemed to her a likely place to get injured if Tori had disappeared on her own, or a place a criminal might have hidden a body if her disappearance had been foul play. It had also been the place where Tori was last seen by another hiker. Right in the middle of the boulder field, according to the report. Either way, no matter how much Jordyn searched it, it had yielded no information. She'd finally given up searching, focused on finding a way to move forward, so she hadn't been back here in a while. It had been enough years that she couldn't quite remember for sure if the boulder field she was thinking of was here or farther ahead. She could look at the GPS coordinates to confirm if she needed to, but right now she just followed Cipher.

A couple hundred yards down the trail, it looked like this was the place she remembered. The boulder field was at the edge of the woods, with a variety of different-sized rocks creating a sort of natural obstacle course. Some of the boulders were small, only a couple of feet across, and some were the size of a small house, or at least a large shed. They were all jumbled together in a mess of boulders that made the terrain difficult to traverse. You could easily roll an ankle if you weren't watching where you were going. It was the three-dimensional equivalent of quicksand—an area that could figuratively suck you in and trap you even though it didn't look too intimidating.

Jordyn watched Cipher closely, ready to pick the dog up and carry her if need be. Ground like this was especially difficult for some dogs to travel, but Cipher had always had a high amount of athleticism and dexterity, so Jordyn thought she'd be okay. Sure enough, the K-9 moved slightly slower, as though she were aware of the dangers, but with the same confidence she always had, until about the middle of the boulder field. Then she whined, but didn't lie down or howl, her usual alert signals. She started to move again, and nothing about her movements suggested injury. Jordyn looked back at Finn, whose face was concerned again. They were committed now, though, and it seemed as though Cipher was speeding up as she moved toward...

A rock up ahead. Huge, low to the ground, and lighter in one area. As Jordyn looked at it longer, she realized the variation in the rock's color wasn't natural; it was the coloring of the clothes of the body lying on the rock. As her mind registered what they'd found, Cipher made it to the body, lay down and howled.

Jordyn, who thought Cipher's alert howl was both gutting and haunting under the best of circumstances, flinched even more than usual. It wasn't a quiet noise, and if someone was in the woods with them, they'd know their location.

While Jordyn had slowed her pace, maybe subconsciously, it seemed that Finn had sped up. He moved past her toward the body, looked down at it then back up at Jordyn.

"It's the most recent missing woman. Nicole Collins."

She glanced over at the body, flinched again, this time at the clear gunshot wound to the woman's forehead. Exactly like the MO had been for every missing woman so far.

"That's what I thought." She said the words even as she felt her stomach clench down in an ache. They were too late to help Nicole, but her family would get some answers. She'd wanted answers for herself, though. She'd wanted to find Tori. She'd told herself it was about their current case, and it had been, but some part of her had wanted to find Tori also.

When was she going to realize that closure wasn't always a thing? That sometimes the only resolution was no resolution at all?

"I'm going to call it in," she told him as she pulled out her radio, trying to ignore the way the skin on the back of her neck was prickling again, like someone was watching her, watching them.

# ELEVEN

As Jordyn radioed in what she'd found, Finn went over his options while he stood looking around them, trying to stay aware of any potential threats since he still didn't feel like it was safe to let his guard down.

Option 1. He could stay "disappeared," but it was going to get complicated after this. He'd been here with Jordyn, at the crime scene. He wasn't going to ask her to lie for him, and probably his footprints were on the trail. His scent definitely was. Were Jordyn and Cipher the only K-9 team being used in the search or were there more?

Option 2. He could come clean, stay here at the crime scene, tell them why he'd disappeared. It would require a lot of trust that he'd be able to be kept safe somehow from whoever had attacked him in the first place, which, given the circumstances, seemed like a risk he wasn't willing to take. His gut was still telling him that someone at the FBI was involved somehow. Trusting the wrong person wasn't a mistake he could afford.

Option 3. He could bide his time, wait and see if they noticed someone else had been here with her. Probably they would, but it was possible he could still stay hidden. This option was the trickiest as it had the most unknowns, the most variables, but it was possibly the best option for him.

It was hard to say. He didn't like the way it would involve asking Jordyn to lie, or at least hide some of the truth. She wouldn't like it either, he suspected.

He watched as Jordyn moved toward the body, saw a frown cross her face.

"What are you doing?" Up until this point, he'd avoided getting too close, and so had she. Instead, they'd been looking at the body from five or so feet away. The way the boulders were arranged placed them on the other side of another big boulder, so that they couldn't see the woods clearly behind them.

"There's a note." She reached forward, and Finn realized that as she did so, she was leaving the accidental shelter of the large boulder, and that there was a straight line of visibility between her and the woods.

"Jordyn, no, get down!" he yelled, gut instinct kicking in as he dived, taking her with him. They both went down as a shot rang out. He noticed Jordyn had reached for Cipher's harness and pulled her close as well.

The noise of the gun's report was quickly followed by a sound Finn was fairly certain was the bullet ricocheting off of the rock they'd just dived behind.

After a moment, he lifted his head up, just barely. He could only see other rocks, no telltale signs of anything like a scope glinting. The shooter was probably in the woods, waiting for the moment one of them would step out into the open to read the note. While it might have been a stretch to immediately assume it was a trap, it was obvious that his assumption had been correct.

He'd been braced for another shot to follow the first, but whoever was out there wasn't an idiot or careless with their shooting. If they were out of range, the shooter wouldn't fire again.

Until they were in range again.

From their position on the ground, it was going to be nearly impossible to tell if someone was approaching them from the woods. And if this was the serial killer after them, as hard as it was to imagine, whoever it was would have no problem walking right up to them and shooting them in the forehead at point-blank range. Which was what the killer had done to all the victims so far.

Finn hated what that meant about his sister's death if this case and Tori's were connected. If that had been his sister's end too, it felt unfair. Rage inducing. Tori hadn't done anything to deserve something like that. But none of these women had. That was what made a criminal like this so terrifying and upsetting, why serial killers were featured in so many books and movies—it wasn't right. It was against the very essence of humanity and how people were supposed to behave. It was wrong.

He wasn't going to let anything happen to Jordyn. The thought was one of the clearest in his mind right now, and he glanced over at her as he tried to figure out what to do next. Her eyes were wide, but her jaw was set in that stubborn way he'd noticed she had when she refused to be defeated. Good. He needed her confident and ready for whatever they were facing. Later, there would be time to fall apart, if that was what she needed. And Finn found himself wanting to be the man who kept her safe physically long enough that she could do that, and made her feel safe enough emotionally that falling apart felt less like coming undone and more like falling into something soft where she could rest.

Head in the game. He looked away from her, worked on formulating his strategy as he took stock of their situation.

The boulder field was essentially a maze. The woods

were the danger zone but also their only hope of safety. If they stayed here for too long, Finn was sure that whoever was shooting at them would come and finish the job face-to-face, and it was a matter of *when* not *if*. They needed to get back to the woods, back to the trail.

Jordyn's supervisor should be on his way by now. Hopefully that would help them, not backfire in some way. He still was hoping to be able to avoid letting the authorities know he was still alive, but right now his main focus was keeping him and Jordyn that way—alive.

"Whoever it is, they're going to come closer," Jordyn whispered to him. She looked over at Cipher. "I can't let her go see where they are because it would put her at too much risk." She looked down. "My phone is buzzing."

"Leave it."

"What if it's my boss?"

He considered, realized she had a point. He nodded toward it, and Jordyn slid it out of her pocket.

"It's a text." She was frowning. "They're not coming yet. It's going to be a few hours."

There went hoping that help was on the way.

"We have to get into the woods." He squeezed his eyes shut as he tried to figure out a plan. If they were careful, it might be possible to make their way across the boulder field with minimum exposure. He thought this idea might have the least amount of risk involved.

But risking Jordyn at all made him sick to his stomach.

"Do you think Cipher can army crawl across? Or at least stay low to the ground?" He knew if there was any risk to the dog, Jordyn wasn't going to do it.

"I think so. I don't see how we have much of a choice." Her jaw was tight, her eyes serious. Finn knew she understood the gravity of the situation.

It would be too easy to lose focus now, to get distracted at how easily they could end up like the other victims, fall into despair instead of doing something to give themselves the best chance of survival.

He reached for her hand and squeezed it. She looked up, surprised, but said nothing. "On three, follow me, okay?" Finn had considered the angle of the shots and thought the person in the front would be in the most danger. He could see in her expression that Jordyn had figured that out too, but she didn't fight him, though the look on her face made it clear that she wanted to. "One…two…three."

He army crawled forward, stomach scraping against the uneven ground, the rocks of various sizes that had all come to rest in this spot. It was weird, he thought in a detached way, that this jumble of rocks that was inherently morally neutral had turned into such a jumble of confusion and darkness to him. When this was over, he never wanted to come back here. The natural beauty couldn't make up for all that had happened here. The place his sister was last seen… if they weren't careful, the last place they'd be seen as well.

He felt the crushing weight on his soul. Discouragement. Darkness.

Crawled forward anyway because he couldn't let Jordyn down.

Seconds felt like minutes as they crawled through the rough terrain. The silence was loud and stretched, temporary, he knew that. As soon as they were within sight again, the shooter would try again.

The explosion of another gunshot rocked him even though he'd been bracing for it. It was almost worse than the first one.

He heard Jordyn let out a yelp, and his heart dropped.

"I'm fine!" she called ahead. "Just scared me. Stupid…"

she muttered something he didn't hear. "Hurry. I want to get out of here!"

Getting out of here was the best idea they'd had all day. Surely better than coming here—that had been a mistake. Or had it? Would someone else have found the body if they hadn't? There had been a note, though neither of them had been able to read what it said. But Finn assumed they were the targets, since whoever was shooting at them could clearly see who they were.

After having been attacked and left for dead, after Jordyn had been run off the road, he knew this wasn't random in the slightest.

The killer wanted them dead.

Jordyn had no idea how Finn was just unflinchingly crawling through the rocks as someone shot at them. She'd have said she had nerves of steel after her time as a SAR worker, as she'd been in plenty of situations that required her to keep her cool in a crisis. She'd always considered it sort of a superpower, but right now she didn't feel that way at all. She felt small and vulnerable. Who could possibly want to murder them? And if Finn was correct—that someone from the FBI was involved—how could someone who knew him, who'd had conversations and looked at him in the face possibly want him dead?

It hurt her mind to contemplate it. She didn't know how people like Finn did their jobs day in and day out, grappling with the reality of evil in the world. She knew it existed, but it didn't often have a face for her. It did for them.

Except not this time. A face would be helpful, some indication of who was behind these attacks would go a long way toward ending them, but right now she felt completely in the dark. Was anyone at the police department closer to figuring out who the culprit was? And why was backup going to take so long? Unless there was another emergency or break in the case, the police should be on their way now.

Jordyn's thoughts raced as they made a measured but excruciatingly slow crawl through the exposed rocks. She guided Cipher, keeping the dog low as well, and tried to find order in her chaotic thoughts. It was something she'd caught herself doing many times, trying to control something she could when life felt like it was spiraling out of her grasp. But she also had to focus on what she was doing.

They were approaching the woods now, the welcome shelter of the trees not far away. Twenty yards? Thirty? The trees were thinner against the edge of the boulder field, but she could tell by the darkness in the forest further in that they'd get thicker. Even though whoever was after them was in those woods somewhere, their chances would be better since there was somewhere to hide, a way to escape.

"Run!" Finn said as they approached the woods. She stood, giving Cipher the command to follow her.

She heard a shot explode behind them but could see Finn moving on one side, Cipher on the other. They were okay. They were really okay.

Finn set a fast pace through the trees. The sun had come out from behind the clouds, causing a strobe effect through the trees as they ran. Light. Dark. Light. Dark. The trees were such a welcome haven, but still not what she'd call hospitable. Their footsteps pounded through the woods as they kept low, and she prayed they could outrun their attacker's bullets. The ground was fairly soft, probably from recent rains. There was a chance that not only would they be able to track their would-be killer's movements by using Cipher's nose, but also with footprints.

The run back to the car felt substantially faster than the

hike up into the woods and then the boulder field had, and for that she was grateful.

No sign of the shooter following them. That was a good sign.

"If your boss is going to be another—" Finn glanced at his watch "—hour or so, do you mind driving me back to your house?"

"No problem."

"I don't think we're going to be able to hide the fact that I was there. Not really. But I want a little more time to think before I talk to anyone from the FBI, and I'm guessing they'll arrive with your boss."

She nodded. He was right. The ground had been soft enough to leave impressions—two clear sets of footprints. The chances of getting out of this day without having to explain to someone why she'd been at a crime scene with someone else and who that someone else was were slim.

But it was better than the police department finding both of their dead bodies in the boulder field.

They climbed into her car, and she started driving.

He was right of course, but somehow the thought of facing everyone without him was overwhelming. Jordyn wanted to laugh at herself. A couple of days in Finn's presence and suddenly she was used to working with a human partner to the degree that it was strange if he wasn't there? That surprised her. She'd been a bit of a loner since Tori died. She'd always been more of a "one best friend" than a group of friends kind of person, and after Tori…she just hadn't…hadn't wanted to make friends? Hadn't had the energy?

Hadn't wanted to risk getting close to someone again, if she were being honest with herself. Losing Tori had hurt

so badly that she knew she had developed a habit of pushing people away.

She glanced over at Finn. Did he do the same? Or was
it just her. How much of their experience and reaction to
the situation had been similar? And would it be too weird
or hard to discuss it with him? It had felt easy earlier. Hard
to talk about, easy to discuss with him. She wanted to talk
to him more.

But surely she wasn't... She struggled to find words.
She wasn't developing feelings for him, was she? At least
it was something harmless and unserious like a crush, not
genuine feelings...right?

She glanced over at him, felt her stomach flutter a little.
It wasn't just missing having a human partner. She was already missing *Finn*, and he wasn't even gone yet.

It was enough to keep her quiet the rest of the drive to
her house.

Waiting in the driveway long enough to ensure that he
was safely inside, hopefully with the door locked, Jordyn
drove back to the trailhead quickly, thankful to see that
there weren't any cars in it. Her heartbeat had noticeably
quickened, anxiety making her breathe a little faster than
usual. If Finn was right, and someone from the FBI was
involved, would she soon be face-to-face with a killer?
She knew it was unrealistic to somehow be able to sense
it. If anyone would have been able to tell, it would be Finn.

Then again, he *had* known hadn't he? At least it seemed
that way. If he'd been in the woods and had confronted the
killer, something had to have led him there. She assumed
he probably couldn't remember what it was, but she'd ask
when she got home, just in case.

In less than half an hour, several cars pulled in. She
watched from her car as they started climbing out of the

vehicles. One of them was a huge black SUV that may as well have had FBI spray-painted on the sides of it in neon pink. It was about as subtle as a moose in rut.

The other vehicle was an Eagle Bend Police Department cruiser. Sergeant Patrick and Officer Lee both got out of his car.

The black SUV held several agents she didn't know but recognized on sight as having been involved in this investigation. As a search and rescue worker, Jordyn had a unique position in a case like this. She knew more about this case than some SAR workers usually knew. Sergeant Patrick had told her from the start that he was reading her in as much as he was allowed because this was more dangerous than anything she'd done for them before, and he wanted her to be fully prepared and on her guard. She appreciated it, as she'd appreciated a lot of things about working for him. Surely he wasn't the killer, right? It had to be someone on the FBI side.

She eyed the three agents who had climbed from the car, noticing they were standing with a fourth person from the Bureau, Melissa, the profiler. The woman was wearing slacks, dress shoes—though at least they appeared to be flats—and a button-down shirt. Not the most practical clothes for trekking through the woods, but Jordyn guessed they'd all come in a hurry, as much as they could have. She was still curious about the delay. A glance at her watch told her it had been just under two hours from when they'd found the body. She knew they'd have wanted to get here as soon as possible.

Bracing herself with a deep breath, Jordyn climbed out of her own vehicle and watched the others. It was a shame she couldn't read the facial expressions of everyone at one time. She'd love to see everyone's individual reaction to the fact that she was here in the parking lot, not up there with the body. When she'd radioed it in, they hadn't been shot at yet. They probably weren't expecting to see her till they reached the boulder field.

Sergeant Patrick did a double take as she walked toward them. She didn't think that it was a faked response, further solidifying her already fairly firm opinion that he wasn't involved at all.

"I assumed you'd stay with the body." His words were even and didn't give away any of the frustration she thought he must be feeling right now.

Jordyn shook her head. "So did I. Until I was shot at."

A quick glance at the faces, one at a time as quickly as she could. Her boss was already surprised, and he looked more so now, as did his partner.

The FBI guys were harder to read. Their faces seemed fairly expressionless as a rule, which made sense. It was probably in their job description. Melissa's face wasn't much better, but again, it always had the same passive expression that was probably supposed to make her seem non-threatening while she stood around analyzing everyone.

"Tell me more." Patrick glanced over at the trailhead then back at Jordyn. "We need to get up there…"

"We can go up ahead and clear the area if you'd like to stay down here with her." One of the FBI guys offered. She glanced at his nametag. Hawkins.

"That would be great, Hawkins," Sergeant Patrick said.

"Actually," Jordyn spoke up. "I would like to hike back up still. I had to leave in a hurry, and Cipher wasn't able to search the whole area."

"But you found the body," one of the other FBI agents said. His last name was Littleton.

"One of them, yes. The most recent woman who was reported missing, I believe." She'd only had a second to look at the deceased, but the description fit. "But it's important that my dog be able to clear the entire area."

Her boss was nodding. "She's right. But we'll go up in the back."

"I'll stay in the back too, if that's okay?" Melissa looked over at the FBI men, who nodded briefly, then over at Sergeant Patrick, who also nodded his approval.

"I'll go with them." Officer Lee offered, flipping her dark brown hair over her shoulder as she walked away.

That left the three of them taking up the rear. Much as the profiler made Jordyn feel too analyzed to be entirely comfortable, she was somewhat thankful that the others were going ahead of them. Logic suggested that the killer was long gone from the area by now, assuming he or she had been lying in wait for them, since they'd clearly left and were no longer targets. But Jordyn still felt uneasy in her stomach when she considered going back to the boulder field. When this was over, she might never return to it. The area held no good memories at all.

"So what happened up there?" Sergeant Patrick asked, and Jordyn gave him a summary the best that she could, while leaving out Finn's involvement. She explained that she'd wanted to go back to Tori's point last seen, on a hunch that it could have something to do with this case somehow. She left out Finn's thought on it possibly being the same killer. Instead, she implied that her thought had been that it could be some kind of copycat and that had made her bring Cipher to search the area. It seemed to make sense to Sergeant Patrick.

"And when you found the body someone shot at you?" he clarified.

"After that. I bent to look at something beside the body. A note, I think."

"A note…" Melissa muttered. Jordyn could practically hear the wheels turning in her mind as she attempted to put together this killer's psychological state. It was a field she'd been briefly interested in herself, thinking maybe she could marry her love of psychology with her desire to help solve crimes like this, but SAR work had been more rewarding than she would have ever anticipated, and once she and Cipher had gotten started, Jordyn hadn't been able to fathom doing any kind of work like this without a dog to help her.

"What did it say?" her boss asked, and Jordyn had to shake her head. She hadn't even realized until they'd been running that she hadn't read the note. Would it still be there? Or would she have to wonder what it said?

"The shooting started just as I was reaching for it."

He didn't say anything, just seemed to be considering what she'd told him. Jordyn appreciated that about him, he wasn't a man who filled empty spaces with words needlessly.

They continued walking in silence. Mostly, Jordyn walked with Cipher, looking at the area around them, trying to make sure that no threat caught them unaware. Now and then she'd glance at Sergeant Patrick, who looked deep in thought, or Melissa, who also seemed to be considering everything Jordyn had said. Occasionally one of them would look at the ground, and Jordyn tried to do so also, mostly to see how much of an impression her and Finn's footprints had left on the ground. Technically anyone could have been on this trail. An extra set of footprints might not be noticed by a normal individual, but everyone here was trained to notice small details like that. The fact that they'd been running was even more of a tell. The footprints would be deeper in the front, lighter in the back, clear indication of a quick escape. She was wearing the same shoes, so her prints would be a clear match.

Jordyn knew there was nothing to be done about it. Either they noticed or they didn't. But her gut gnawed as she waited to see if they were going to say anything. She knew Finn didn't want her to lie for him, and her integrity and faith in Jesus wouldn't allow her to anyway. But she didn't know what she would say if they called her out on it. Even though the shooter would have seen Finn, and the fact that he was alive was no longer a secret, at least to the person they most needed to conceal it from, she still hesitated to let anyone know for sure that he was alive. Until she knew who she could trust, she didn't want to trust anyone. Besides, what if the shooter had only seen two people and didn't know for sure one of them was Finn? No, she couldn't give up his secret, not with the amount of risk it would carry. She needed Finn to be okay. For many reasons. Several of which she wasn't ready to explore yet.

As the boulder field finally came into view, she found her breathing getting shallow, involuntarily, as her chest tightened. It took effort to breathe deeply in, expand her chest and try to push past the feelings of anxiety that were wrapping themselves around her like tendrils of fear, but she made herself do it. Anxiety wasn't going to bring Tori or Nicole Collins back or help them or catch whoever was behind this. She whispered a quick prayer for help. While she didn't doubt that God heard her and cared, it wasn't like she felt better instantly. Instead, she took a deep breath and decided she was going to have to do it afraid.

She and Cipher took the lead, and Jordyn found herself thankful that the other FBI agents had been out here already, had cleared the scene to some degree. She didn't

know if she was a target at all at this point, or if it was only
Finn. Probably she was too, considering the running-off-
the-road incident, but it was possible they'd only wanted to
find Finn and somehow had figured out that Jordyn knew
where he was.

Impossible to say. She needed to stay on guard either
way. Chills running down her back, she took a deep breath
and started to weave her way back through the boulders.

# TWELVE

This morning had messed Finn up. He tried to ignore how empty Jordyn's house felt without her in it. First, he was more aware than ever of how much of a target he was—how much of a target they *both* were. This was more than a killer who didn't want to get caught, at least he thought so. It spoke of someone who had a lot to lose, a desperation that wasn't unhinged but instead was calculated, well planned.

This killer was intelligent, not motivated by passion, he thought. He'd seen Melissa Reynolds work enough in her job as a profiler that Finn was under no illusions he could do that kind of work himself, after all she'd been specially trained, but he did understand to a degree the way that she picked apart scenes and suspects to predict future events in a case, which he was trying to do now.

His command center was Jordyn's kitchen table. He'd helped himself to a cup of coffee and spread out papers on the desk. He'd risked borrowing a bike he found in Jordyn's garage and heading back to his old apartment to grab his case files, which included his notes from this case as well as everything the FBI had on Tori's disappearance. It had seemed like a foolish decision in some ways, but the only logical choice in others. At least Jordyn hadn't been with him, that was part of his rationalization, and things

seemed to be escalating to the point where he wasn't sure
how wise it was to continue to hide anyway. Whoever was
after him was after her now too. As far as Finn was concerned, the clock was ticking, leaving him little time to
solve this. One of these times that they were shot at, the
killer wasn't going to miss.

Back in Jordyn's house, reasonably certain he'd not been
followed, he'd locked himself back in. Every moment he
wasn't in hiding was another moment he was risking discovery.

Finn had never intended to look at his sister's case when
he got access to the files at the Eagle Bend Police Department, not really. He was under no delusions that he'd somehow be able to piece it together. He'd joined the FBI so other
families wouldn't feel that kind of pain, not because he felt
any assurance that he'd be able to give his own family some
closure. He never even told his parents, who moved to Seattle not long after the case was declared cold, unable to cope
with the reminders of their daughter, that he had access to
the files. It wouldn't have done any good.

He'd never even looked at the files until recently, he realized now as he flipped through them again, another part
of his memory returning. The date accessed, according to
the computer database he'd logged into at the Eagle Bend
Police Department, which was printed on the edges of the
copies, was only a week ago.

What had made him open it then? That he couldn't remember, not really. It was close, like it was creeping forward in his mind, but not close enough to grasp yet.

Something in the current case…

He stood up from the table, walked around the house.
He'd look at it all again, every single missing woman who
the FBI was currently tying to the serial killer. And then

he'd reread Tori's case files. Then he'd keep doing both. Because something in his mind was convinced the two were connected.

Today's discovery seemed to affirm that. Why else would the body have been in the same boulder field where Tori had been last seen? It was tied together somehow, he could feel it. He just wasn't sure how. Or why.

Or most importantly, *who* was behind any of it.

Breathing seemed to work slightly better the longer Jordyn was exposed in the boulder field and not being shot at, like her body had finally acknowledged that just because she'd been in danger here before, didn't mean that she was in danger here right now.

She still flinched, though, when one of the FBI agents who stood near the body reached down to pick up the paper she knew was the note. But nothing happened. No gunshot pierced the silence this time, there was just the silent, cool mountain air and stillness all around them. It wasn't even that eerie stillness that was almost too still. It just felt... fine. Normal.

The way life went on in places like this, where tragedy and senseless violence had occurred, was hard to fathom. The views were still beautiful, but evil had taken place here, just like she'd thought at the other site Cipher had found. It was a discordant note in her mind.

"What does it say?" Sergeant Patrick asked the FBI agents before she had a chance to.

"Leave the past where it belongs." The one who was holding the note in his gloved hand frowned. "So did some-one intend for someone specific to find this?" he asked, the question clearly rhetorical among a group of people who were either law enforcement or law enforcement affiliated and all wondering he same thing.

"I don't like that at all," Officer Lee muttered, her jaw tight.

"Whoever killed her moved her here from somewhere else," the second FBI agent commented from the ground. He motioned to some light stains on the rock. "The blood left evidence."

"Always does," Melissa muttered. Jordyn didn't know if she meant literally or metaphorically, though she supposed either was true. It seemed like something a psychologist would say.

It was silent for a moment or two as they started to process the scene. Jordyn was standing a little apart, not really part of this. She noticed Melissa was doing the same, but she was looking around. Trying to see this through the eyes of the killer?

Jordyn should probably focus on her own job before she drew too much attention to herself by standing there watching. She was pretty sure that harboring Finn wasn't illegal. It wasn't as though they'd said they were investigating him and she was specifically obstructing justice or anything. But his safety could depend on remaining off the radar. She spoke up. "I'll take Cipher around the boulder field and see if she alerts on anything else."

Her boss nodded and she wandered away from them, Cipher at her side. She gave her the command to search, and the dog did so, stopping occasionally to investigate an area further but not alerting on anything specific. Until they were at the edge of the boulder field, back near the trail where they'd come in, but a little farther to the west edge of the woods. Then the K-9's demeanor seemed to change, much like it had earlier.

She glanced over at where the body was and saw that Sergeant Patrick had noticed Cipher's behavior and was moving in her direction.

"What did she find?" he asked.

"Not sure yet. But possibly the location where the shooter was."

From where she was now, she could see lots of footprints in the dirt, but she did feel like hers and Finn's stuck out more. At this point, the rest of the dirt was a jumble of the FBI agents' tracks, Officer Lee's tracks, Melissa's tracks, Sergeant Patrick's...their shooter likely wouldn't be as trackable as he or she would have been earlier, but Jordyn knew that investigating earlier would not have been an option. Not unless they'd wanted to be killed.

"So that's Nicole Collins. The missing woman," Sergeant Patrick said.

Jordyn nodded. "I believe so."

Jordyn hurt for Nicole's family even though she didn't know them.

"I'll have the guys come over and search this area for evidence the shooter left behind. There's got to be something." She could hear the frustration in his voice and understood how he felt. It was long past time for them to figure out who was behind this. "You can go ahead and head back. We didn't see any signs of trouble on the way up, so I'm thinking you'll be okay. But listen, that note was intended for someone, and if it was for you, you need to be careful."

"Do you really think it could have been targeted at me?" she asked.

"I don't see why, but if the person shooting at you had any kind of scope or powerful sight, they should have been able to tell who you were. It's possible it was random." He paused as though weighing his words. "It doesn't appear

that the victims have anything obvious in common or link-
ing them in any way." He appeared to consider again. "It
could be random. I wish I knew. You'd better be careful,
just in case."

Jordyn didn't need any more convincing. She was already planning to be watchful, after all the other things that
had happened today, but she didn't know how to tell him
that without telling him about Finn. But without knowing
exactly what had convinced Finn that he couldn't trust his
coworkers at the FBI, she couldn't jeopardize his safety.
So she just nodded then called Cipher to her and started
back down the trail.

She'd been walking for five or so minutes when she
started to jog. It wasn't that she felt like someone was
watching her, not specifically. It was more that she was
spooked just being out here, uncertain in a place that had
once been where she'd felt the most confident. Looking
around yielded nothing obvious to be concerned about,
but she still didn't slow her pace. She was more than ready
to get out of here.

By the time she finally made it to her car, her body felt
as worn down as her mind, and all she wanted was to get
home. When she got there, she noticed bike tires on the
driveway.

She couldn't remember the last time she'd ridden a bike.
Her heart dropped into her stomach. Finn.

With Cipher running beside her, she ran the short distance from the driveway to the front door, fumbling a little
with her key as she struggled to make her hands still enough
to get it in the lock. Anything could have happened to him
in the time that she'd been gone. And losing him wouldn't
just mean losing her last link to Tori. It meant losing someone she considered a friend.

Maybe someone she'd hoped would be more than a friend eventually.

His face flashed in her mind, his eyes kind, mouth smiling, jaw shadowy with stubble.

At the moment, she couldn't even consider the possibility of such a thing, her mind wouldn't allow her to as self-protective instincts took over. Finn was very likely in trouble, or worse, so imagining a future with him was...

The key finally settled into the lock, and she turned it, hurrying into the house.

She rounded the corner into the living room, wishing she could call his name, but not wanting to alert anyone else who could be in the house to her presence.

Then her eyes landed on him. Sitting at the dining room table. Perfectly fine.

"Finn!" This time his name did escape from her lips, but instead of the desperation she was sure he would have heard in her tone only moments before, now it was filled with frustration and annoyance and...and relief.

"What?" He shoved his chair back and walked into the living room, where she was standing, having stopped when she saw him. "You okay, Jordyn?"

"I thought...there were bike tracks. I thought someone had been here. But you're fine?" She asked it because even though she could see with her own eyes that it was true, she somehow wasn't quite sure of herself.

"I'm fine."

His voice was steadying to her, and she felt her muscles relax even as her heartbeat quickened. They were a few feet apart, and Jordyn stepped forward, closing the distance between them. She was going to kiss him, wasn't she? It wasn't something she'd planned, but she knew that was where this was leading.

And all she could think was *finally*. Her eyes dipped to his lips. Back up to his eyes.

Jordyn thought Finn's eyes might have widened a little, but he didn't move either. Until right before she was about to close her eyes and finally let herself have a glimpse of what she'd been missing all these years. Pounding on the door made them both jump apart, eye contact broken as they both turned toward the door.

# THIRTEEN

Finn should have been more surprised than he was by the knock on the door. Of course something would interrupt that moment they were finally about to have.

"Go. Hide." Jordyn's voice was breathless. From their near kiss? Or whoever was at the door—almost certainly law enforcement.

"They know I'm here. Almost certainly." He felt like the voice of reason, though he appreciated her concern for him. But he left the room anyway.

"Sergeant Patrick." Jordyn's voice carried from the living room. He could hear clearly from his hiding place in the hall closet. "Officer Lee. And you guys too. Agent Littleton, Agent Hawkins. Melissa. Long time no see."

He didn't hear any response to the weak joke and had a feeling it had fallen as flat as it sounded.

"We have a problem, Jordyn."

"A problem?"

"Ever heard of obstructing justice?" Melissa's voice was calm, almost bored. The same voice she used when she was analyzing a suspect. Surely she didn't consider Jordyn to be one?

"Definitely something I've heard of but not something I make a habit of doing," Jordyn said.

"That's what I told them..." Sergeant Patrick's voice trailed off a little, and Finn had to struggle to hear. Then it got louder again. "But we saw the tracks, Jordyn. Someone else was there with you."

"There are plenty of tracks on that trail..." she replied.

Everyone in the room had to know that was a lame excuse. Finn eased around the corner, heading for the front door. If he was right and someone from the case wanted him dead, word would almost certainly get back to them if he walked into the room with all those people in it. He'd have to watch his back. But people were running them off the road and shooting at them now, so how much worse could it be, realistically?

"You need to tell us what you know, Jordyn," came Officer Lee's voice. "We need to solve this case." Her voice had an urgency in it that Finn felt to his core. He'd thought he and Jordyn were the only ones who felt so personally invested in the case, but it shouldn't surprise him that the police officers who lived in this town and had sworn to protect it would also feel passionate about righting the wrongs that were taking place in their hometown.

"It was my fault," Finn said, careful to keep his hands out of his pockets where they could see them. As he expected, when he came around the corner, both of the FBI agents tensed, hands moving to their weapons, but when their quick visual assessment showed him to be unarmed, they put their hands down.

He didn't miss the way Sergeant Patrick's eyes darted to Jordyn, gauging her reaction, most likely. Her face gave nothing away, which impressed him. The man then looked back at Finn.

"I suggest you explain what you're doing here and where you've been, as you're currently a person of interest in this case," he said slowly, still watching for trouble, or so it appeared to Finn.

"There's got to be an explanation for that. Why would I be a person of interest?"

"You disappear without warning in the middle of a case right when another woman turns up missing?" Agent Hawkins spoke. "Right after leaving a note like the one on your desk?"

"Note?" Finn glanced over at Jordyn, needing to make sure she still believed him. Her eyes still looked calm, her jaw tight. Nothing about her looked suspicious of him. For that he was thankful, anyway.

"There was a note in your apartment. A ransom demand addressed to Nicole Collins's parents."

"That doesn't even make sense. This killer doesn't leave ransom notes." And in his apartment?

"Unless the MO has changed," Melissa spoke up.

"And I'm not the killer," Finn said, conviction firm in his voice.

Sergeant Patrick, Officer Lee, Agent Hawkins and Agent Littleton were staring at him.

"It wasn't my note. I didn't write it. Or kill anyone. Someone must have planted it there. Check the handwriting, has anyone done that yet?" Though he didn't know why. What good did it do to shift suspicion onto him?

"Visually, it's a match. But it hasn't been confirmed by analysis, not yet. Lab is backed up," Agent Littleton admitted.

"I don't think Finn is lying," Melissa said, her voice calm and certain.

"That's all well and good, but until we know for sure, we need to treat him as a person of interest. I don't want anything slipping through the cracks in this case," Sergeant Patrick spoke up.

"He's not lying. I'm sure of it. And I don't think he fits the profile. I never thought that, even after the note was found."

The four law enforcement officers—two Eagle Bend PD, two FBI—eyed each other. Melissa didn't comment but seemed to be watching everyone else's movements. Her eyes missed nothing, though.

Sergeant Patrick still looked suspicious. Finn felt Jordyn's eyes on him, noted the way she glanced up at his head where it was injured, her eyes asking whether or not she could tell them what she'd seen. He nodded.

"He was attacked, Sergeant." Jordyn spoke up, addressing her boss. "I don't see how he could be a person of interest when I found him unconscious in a clearing in the woods, with a head injury that could have killed him."

That seemed to get his attention. The other man raised his eyebrows, his face slightly less suspicious, his jaw slightly more relaxed.

"Explain."

"Jordyn and I are old friends. We knew each other in high school," Finn started, looking over at Jordyn. He'd decided earlier that he was going to have to be honest with the others working this case, but that didn't mean they needed every single detail. Sharing how Cipher alerted on him because there had been a body there, talking about Jordyn's role in getting him out of the wilderness and to her house…he wasn't sure those things were necessary, so he was going to stick to the basics that were true and needed.

"When you came to my office," Sergeant Patrick's words were directed at Jordyn, "you knew he was here?"

He'd been planning to take the lead for the entire rest of

the conversation, but he couldn't very well answer things for her when she was being asked directly, or it was going to look even worse than if she shared more of the story than he thought was a good idea to share.

Jordyn nodded. "I did."

And that was all she said. He admired her restraint. Most people's instinct was to say too much. She played her cards close to the vest. Of course, he should have guessed that, as that was also inherent in a lot of her personality, it seemed.

"Jordyn agreed to let me stay here after I was attacked." He brushed back some of his hair, which revealed the scab from one of the gashes on the side of his head.

That appeared to do a lot to further prove his innocence. Immediately, both FBI agents were on the phone, and Melissa was making notes in a notebook, periodically hmming as she did so.

"Why not tell someone?" Sergeant Patrick looked at both of them.

"It didn't seem safe." Jordyn spoke up before he could say anything. "Not when he was injured the way he was."

"Concussion?" Patrick asked.

"Nothing official," Finn said, not wanting word of the extent of his injury to get back to the killer if someone in the room really did have connections to whoever had attacked him.

"Why didn't you report whatever happened to you?" Melissa asked in that quiet voice of hers.

Both FBI agents especially looked interested in his answer, and Finn understood it. It was a massive breech of protocol, and if there was one thing the FBI held close to its heart, it was protocol.

"It didn't seem prudent," he said, offering nothing else. No one commented, and he felt his heartbeat slow a little.

"You're going to have to give a statement," Sergeant Patrick said.

"I'm prepared to do that."

Silence again. Finn could tell that the other man didn't trust him fully. That suited him fine, as he wasn't inclined to trust anyone either right now. But he understood that ultimately this was Sergeant Patrick's case. His town, his jurisdiction. The FBI was here in an advisory capacity, to help with the case and supplement law enforcement presence and manpower, not to take over. That was why the FBI agents were hanging back, letting Sergeant Patrick make the calls.

"Here or at the station?" Jordyn asked.

"Let's go ahead and go in," Sergeant Patrick suggested.

Finn and Jordyn loaded into her car without a word, not needing to even discuss the fact that they were riding together, which seemed to be fine with everyone else. Finn tried to make sense of what the others might be thinking based on this. Clearly they didn't think he was a flight risk, or they'd have taken more precautions to ensure he showed up where he was supposed to be. That was good. Sergeant Patrick might not fully trust him, but he must at least a little, or he wouldn't have let him ride with Jordyn without someone else in the car.

He couldn't get a handle on what his coworkers were thinking. But that felt fair, since he didn't know what he thought about them either. Melissa was always so quiet, judgmental probably without meaning to be. Agent Hawkins was the strong and silent type, a quintessential FBI agent. He usually gave the impression that he'd just as soon disappear someone as go through questioning them if they really were guilty. Agent Littleton was new to the Anchorage field office, and from what Finn had observed over the last year or so working with him, he was a bit more new school, extremely by the book to the point where he sometimes hesitated when he shouldn't. They only represented some of the agents who were involved in liaising with the Eagle Bend Police Department over this case. It wasn't field-office wide, but there were several other agents who had worked on this case as well, some of whom Finn knew fairly well and some of whom he didn't.

The killer could be any one of them, and anyone could also be unintentionally passing information on to the killer. It was why it was better to err on the side of saying too little.

Finn kept that in mind as he and Jordyn walked into the Eagle Bend Police Department. The amount of people who did a double-take when they saw him was surreal.

All of that must have transpired because of the note they'd found. He knew he hadn't written it, hadn't killed anyone, and the evidence should support that. Melissa and Jordyn backing him up added credence to his claims too. But Finn still disliked feeling so out of control of his own life and freedom. He could only hope Sergeant Patrick was as intelligent a man as he seemed. Sorting through what he could say and shouldn't say, Finn followed the man into his office. Jordyn and the three FBI employees started to follow them in, but Sergeant Patrick held up a hand.

"I'd rather speak to Agent McDaniel alone."

Jordyn caught his eye, and Finn tried to nod slightly without it being obvious. It wasn't as though he had a huge choice in the matter.

"I'll meet you at the car," he said, hoping to reassure her it wouldn't take long.

Jordyn shook her head. "I'm going to go get a cup of coffee in the break room. I'll be in there when you're ready to leave."

She and the others walked away, and Finn stepped into the office, relieved not to be in hiding anymore, and growing more and more anxious that his decision to keep his whereabouts under wraps was going to come back to bite him.

The lukewarm coffee was doing nothing to sooth Jordyn's nerves. She'd considered herself fairly tough for handling the situation the way she had so far, but now that Finn was back here, it was proving to be too much. First, the collision of the world she'd inhabited for the last few days, where she and Finn were friends and the closest of coworkers, and the normal world of their teen years where they avoided each other at all costs. The change was startling. Second, it was like the fallout of an adrenaline rush. She'd known for days that she had to keep him hidden, that the cost could be high if he was discovered, and now suddenly he was out in the open. Something else to adjust to.

Everyone's reactions to him had been fascinating. It had been mostly Sergeant Patrick's she'd paid attention to, since he was her boss and the one she was most interested in clearing as a suspect in the attack on Finn. So far, nothing in his behavior gave anything suspicious away.

But if Tori's death was connected to this, then whoever was responsible had been killing for over five years. Surely by now they'd be fairly adept at avoiding suspicion. So why the rash of killings recently?

Jordyn pulled out her phone whenever anyone else entered the staff room, attempting to look busy. She was in no mood to talk to anyone. Once Officer Lee had walked in, and something in the other woman's face had made Jordyn think she was about to either ask her something or confide in her, but then she'd walked away without speaking. Officer Lee couldn't be involved, could she? Jordyn tried to sort through the encounters they'd had. It could have been a woman who'd run her off the road, who'd shot at them... Nothing said it had to be a man. To Jordyn, the female officer seemed invested in solving the case and didn't strike her as someone who would be on the wrong side of the law at all. But what did she know? Someone wasn't what they seemed, and without knowing who, Jordyn trusted no one but herself and Finn. Well, and her dog, obviously. Cipher lay by her side.

It was just over twenty minutes since they'd come in—she'd checked the time on her phone enough times—when Finn entered.

"Ready?" he said.

She nodded wordlessly and started straight for the parking lot, aware she was probably walking too fast. A couple of times she glanced behind her to make sure Finn was still following, and he was. She kept going, sparing a smile or a nod in someone's direction only if she was directly spoken to.

"You okay?" Finn asked after she'd gotten Cipher settled in the back and they'd climbed into the car.

Jordyn leaned back onto the headrest and blew out a breath. "Yes. No." She shook her head. "Are you okay? Did he believe you?"

"I think so. He let me walk out of there."

Jordyn had so much more she wanted to ask, but now didn't seem like the time to pepper him with questions. She didn't want him to feel like he was facing yet another interrogation. And she needed a distraction from the stress of the last few hours, somewhere productive to focus her energy. "Let's go somewhere. Surely there's something we can do while we wait to see if the lab finds anything useful from the site where we found the body." It was a strange feeling, suddenly having no one to search for after months of almost always being on call. If history repeated itself, she and Cipher wouldn't have more than a week off before another young woman went missing.

It was eerie to consider. Someone was living her life right now, going about her business, unaware that she could be the next victim on a serial killer's list. Unless the killer was stopped—and fast. They didn't have any time to waste.

"Do you mind heading north, toward Cooper Landing?"

The small town Finn referenced was less than an hour from Eagle Bend. Known for its fishing lodges and picturesque location on the famous turquoise Kenai River, Cooper Landing had also been the home of the parents of one of the women who had disappeared. Jordyn knew that because one of the things she'd been doing on her phone in the lounge was reading all of the old news stories about the recent string of missing women. Six in total. Not counting Tori. So possibly seven.

"Are you going to talk to Leah Caldwell's parents?" she asked as she pulled out of the parking lot and started driving in that direction.

"Not necessarily, but I thought we'd check out places from this case that have significance, you know? Anything we can think of."

"Do you have the time to do that? Aren't you working again?"

"I'm still working now," he said with a smile. Then a shadow passed over his face. "But I'm only sort of working now. I get the sense your boss wants to talk to my boss before any decisions are made, so he told me to lie low today, not to leave town. I'm almost entirely cleared of suspicion. But they want that *almost* part nailed down for sure. Handwriting results should come in later today and then our bosses will talk, and I should be good. Sergeant Patrick seemed satisfied with my explanation of the attack. I think he's just being extra cautious waiting for the lab results."

"That's good, though, right? If he's being so careful about you, it means they're starting to be suspicious of everyone, which is functionally what we need, right?"

"I hadn't looked at it that way, but yeah. I guess so. Though admittedly the note is part of what made them suspicious of me."

She thought his expression looked a little lighter then, his jaw slightly less tense.

"I think we should stop somewhere that seems significant in each of the women's lives, see what we can learn. Or go to the place they were found. Or a combination. I'm tossing ideas out here, but I just feel like we have to be close to something, and I have no idea how to go about finding out what."

She could hear the frustration in his voice and didn't know if it was from his head injury and not being able to fully access all the parts of his memory he wanted, or if it was frustration with this case as a whole. Jordyn could fully understand either one. "So Leah Caldwell. Then who?" He wasn't going in order, if he'd started with her. She'd been number…three or four to disappear?

"You drive, I'll make a list."

They drove in silence, which made Jordyn relax more than she'd been able to in days. She watched the scenery pass by through the car windows, the familiar blues and greens of Alaska bringing some level of calm to her over-stimulated mind.

"Okay," Finn finally said.

"Whatcha got?"

"Leah Caldwell was actually farthest out from town. She didn't live in Eagle Bend even though she worked there. I wanted to start with her because she was the farthest out of town. We'll work our way in to other significant locations hopefully making our way back into town later today."

"So where do you want to go for Leah? Point last seen? Areas of significance? Where she was found? Keeping in mind I don't know where any of those places are."

"But didn't you find her?"

"I don't keep all that in my head. I'm not law enforcement, remember? I just find them. Well, Cipher does really."

"I know she's amazing, but you give her too much credit. I've watched you, you're still making decisions about where to take her and what to ask for. So in my book, you're pretty amazing too."

His words warmed her heart, but she didn't know how to respond. It wasn't as though men had been lining up recently to give her compliments. And this affected her more than if they had anyway, because it wasn't just any man saying this about her...it was Finn. The man she was starting to care for—whether that was good for her heart or not.

# FOURTEEN

"To answer your question, though," Finn said, mostly to distract himself from whatever had passed between him and Jordyn when he'd called her amazing, "I thought we'd go to her point last seen. It's a trail not far from the road, it seemed like a good place to start."

Jordyn was nodding along. She was so beautiful. Maybe he should stop trying to distract himself from what he was starting to feel toward her and just…what? Ask how she felt about having a relationship with a man who hadn't decided yet if he wanted to stay in Alaska or move thousands of miles from where Jordyn called home? It wouldn't be fair to her. Or to him. He'd avoided relationships his entire adult life, mostly because he'd been married to his job, and that left no time to date.

What an awful thing to offer a woman—a relationship with a workaholic who may or may not ever be able to move past his own guilt that he hadn't been able to protect his sister from whatever harm had come to her.

Finn felt in some ways like he'd been living in the shadow of her death for years. Jordyn was too full of life to be pulled into that shadow. That was no kind of life for her.

"That sounds good," she said in response to what he'd said, and Finn had to think back. Leah's point last seen.

He nodded again. He could do this, could think of her as a friend and nothing more.

It was growing more difficult, though. She was everything he would ever have thought to look for in a woman and more. She was beautiful, obviously, but that didn't even touch on the other things she admired about her, like how capable she was on a search, how impressive he found it that she could follow Cipher and interpret her signals the way she could. She was confident and smart, and the way they worked together was unlike anything he'd experienced with anyone before. She would be the ideal kind of partner in every way that mattered. Not just in work, but in life. He was…he was falling for her. Hard. But nothing about the circumstances made pursuing anything romantic ideal.

No, better for her if he just kept on ignoring the chemistry between them, though a small part of his mind wondered what it would have been like if the knock at the door earlier hadn't interrupted that almost kiss.

He should just kiss her now. Ask her to pull the car over, tell her how he felt and kiss her, or at least give her another chance to kiss him. With no interruptions this time. But they kept driving.

While reason tried to remind him that he was doing the right thing, a small part of his brain called him a coward, and Finn wondered if it was right. Loving was a risk. Love people and they could leave. Losing a sister was different than if he fell in love with Jordyn and she decided she didn't want to stay. The situations weren't at all comparable. Except losing someone was losing someone, and Finn didn't know if he could take losing anyone else. Better to keep his life more manageable. Controllable.

"It's here," he finally said when they pulled off at the Twin Lakes trailhead. Jordyn parked, and she and Cipher climbed from the car and, like they'd done so many other times, started to search.

An hour later, it was clear that if there had been anything here, there was nothing now. It was a night-and-day difference to the way he was used to seeing Cipher work. She didn't alert on anything, but even more stark was the difference in how she held herself through the entire search. He'd assumed it was a clear-cut "found something" or "haven't found anything," but there were nuances in the husky's behavior he never would have been able to predict. Cipher's body language was relaxed this time, even though she was still obviously working. But her muscles seemed looser, her nose was lifted, but never very much, and her tongue hung out. She looked more like a dog going for a hike.

His disappointment must have shown on his face when they climbed back into the car because Jordyn reached over and put a hand on his arm. "It's okay," she told him, and it was everything he could do not to look over at where she was touching him. His heart skipped a little when she'd put her hand there.

He sounded ridiculous, even to himself. Maybe this was an argument for taking the transfer out of state after all. He wanted to stay and see where this relationship could take them, even if it was just friendship. But it would be all too easy to fall head over heels for her and never recover.

"Where to next?" she asked, a smile on her face, once again being there to offer hope when it would have been his instinct to grow discouraged.

It was something of a wild-goose chase, admittedly. But he admired the fact that she was game.

"Laurie Donaldson," he said. "The place where her body was found."

"Are you thinking maybe Tori's body is in one of these

places? Is that what we're looking for?" she asked him as he drove in that direction.

Finn nodded. "Does that sound crazy?"

"Nah." She laughed a little. "We've seen a lot of crazy things in the past few days, but this doesn't seem like one of them." Then her expression sobered. "Besides, since we found the most recent body at Tori's point last seen, it does seem like it would be worth revisiting these locations. If the serial killer is sort of tangling cases together, it's just as logical a place to search as anything else." They both knew this wasn't just about closure over Tori but also solving this case before anyone else got hurt.

She got it. And he felt like she really did. He'd never felt so much like someone understood him.

What were the chances he would ever feel like this again if he let her walk away?

Focus. He had to focus.

They drove for twenty minutes or so back toward town. Laurie's body had been found at a popular walking trail that wound its way around a lake. Cipher searched the area, and it looked remarkably like the previous search. Her body language was the same, and while Finn tried to hold out hope, he felt pretty quickly like he knew what the results of this search were going to be.

The next few searches yielded the same. Nothing at all.

As they climbed back into the car from the latest unfruitful search, he leaned back against the headrest and closed his eyes. What to try next? It hadn't been a bad idea, he was sure of that. They were close… "What if…" He started talking before the thought had fully formed. "What if we're focusing too much on the others?"

"As opposed to Tori? But we've searched her point last

seen. And obviously if we knew where her body was, we'd have found it by now."

"But we haven't searched her favorite places. For the others, we were talking about searching places of significance too. Maybe we should have done that with Tori."

"They did, during the initial search."

"Well, they didn't have you and Cipher," he insisted. And he wasn't trying to flatter her. He was willing to admit that he'd once not thought search dogs were that helpful, and he'd seen the error of his ways in general. But he still thought that probably Cipher was special, better than many of the other dogs. And as far as he was concerned, Jordyn was impressively attuned both to her dog and their surroundings. No one could search better.

"Where did you have in mind?" she asked in a voice that said she had confidence in him.

He was fully falling for her already, whether he wanted to be or not. He couldn't decide if that terrified him or not.

"Canyon Falls Creek. Tori loved it," Finn said with confidence.

"It was searched," she said flatly. She had hoped that Finn might have a new idea, somewhere that Jordyn knew hadn't been gone over with a fine-toothed comb, like the trails near Canyon Falls Creek had been. It was hostile terrain, slick with water from the waterfall and steep with cliffs and mud. She'd not been part of the initial search because she hadn't had the necessary qualifications to rappel into the canyon, which was where they'd focused most of the search.

As she thought that, she was forced to admit to herself that it was possible the area near the creek might still yield something. They'd hit dead ends everywhere else so far, so they certainly weren't losing anything by following up on this hunch of Finn's.

Jordyn said it aloud. "Canyon Falls Creek. Maybe we should take Cipher and go…" She looked over at him, loving the spark she saw in his eyes.

Loving?

Earlier, when she'd thought he'd been killed and had walked inside her house to find him alive and well, sitting at the table, she'd blamed the rush of feelings on relief. But right now she didn't have any such excuse. At the moment, it was just the two of them in the car, along with her dog, and his eyes were sparkling because he'd had an idea and she thought it was a good one. Suddenly she wanted to chase down this lead for him. In all of her focus on herself and what she'd lost, had she appreciated enough that he had lost a family member? Finn was just as haunted by this case as she was. Jordyn thought back to when he'd been asleep that first night and she'd checked on him because of his head injury. How many of his fitful dreams were recalling the attack that had gotten him injured and how many had been about his sister?

The past relentlessly chased both of them. But right now, for once, she didn't want to think about the past.

"Hey, Finn…" She trailed off. Jordyn didn't have anything to say anyway. She couldn't focus on anything except Finn, his nearness, how much she wanted to kiss him. But she'd already moved close to him. And she'd been the one to move toward him in the house.

Jordyn wasn't moving any further this time.

But Finn, who had seemed this entire time like he just wanted to pretend nothing was happening between them, was looking into her eyes in such a way that Jordyn wasn't sure if he was still trying to pretend at all, or if he was ready to face that something was going on. They'd never been friends, not really, until now. But now they were friends. And maybe…more?

He was going to kiss her, she was sure of it.

As he moved closer, Jordyn found herself thinking that if she'd felt this way about any of the men she'd tried to date in the last few years, maybe she'd have let her guard down a little, tried to get close to someone again. But maybe that was part of what was special about Finn—that she hadn't *meant* to let him past the protective layers she'd built over her heart, and yet here they were.

"What were you saying?" Finn asked, his voice quiet, almost a whisper.

"Nothing." Her heart was beating faster. "I was just…" Her voice trailed off again.

"Do you think…what if…" Finn whispered, moving even closer, his eyes clearly flickering to her lips.

"Yes." They wouldn't be able to go back from this. It was a point of no return.

But as Finn leaned the rest of the way in, closed the distance between them and covered her lips with his, Jordyn had no desire to return to wherever they'd been before.

He kissed like he did everything else in his life. Careful. Confident.

When he moved away, put space between them, her mind spun in a swirl strong enough she was almost dizzy. Jordyn moved in again, kissed him back, and it was clear to her that this wasn't a crush. This had nothing to do with when they were younger and she had a crush on her friend's brother. The fact that he'd been off-limits had nothing to do with the way she admired his dedication to his job, the way he'd been so determined to keep her safe.

When she finally broke the kiss, he muttered "wow"

so quietly she almost didn't hear it, but she did, and she laughed.

"Wow?"

"I mean…" He was shaking his head, eyes wide, blinking like he couldn't quite believe what had just happened between them.

Neither could she.

The practical implications of the kiss rushed at her. How could she fall for someone in law enforcement? Talk about a profession where so much was out of someone's control. Finn would not fit the perfect image of happily-ever-after that she'd created somewhere along the line, where she was a preschool teacher and she married a man who owned the town hardware store or something safe. Anything that would have been at home in a made-for-TV movie.

Never mind that she was far from a preschool teacher and would be bored in a life like that.

Maybe that meant that wasn't the kind of happily-ever-after she really wanted?

At the moment, Jordyn was willing to rewrite any dreams or goals she'd had if it meant having Finn in her life.

"I know we're both stressed," he said, and she felt like his eyes were searching hers. "It doesn't mean…" He cleared his throat. "I don't want to mess anything up."

Jordyn thought about her life now, meals eaten on her couch while she watched TV, wishing she hadn't isolated herself to the point that she had.

"I don't either," she said, feeling a squeeze in her stomach that felt very much like rejection. Because that was what it came down to, didn't it? They were too similar—too comfortable in their self-imposed isolation and too driven by their work. His job would take him away from her soon enough. The least she could do was allow them both to save some face and not go confessing to him that she'd never felt this way about anyone and that she was worried she was already half in love with him. "We're definitely both stressed. It was probably a mistake. Totally my fault," she said, holding up a hand when his face had started to look panicked. The last thing she needed was for him to think she was blaming him for it. He may have started the first kiss, technically, but she'd been the one to move first.

Again.

Honestly, what was the use of protecting her heart and emotions for years only to throw out all of her common sense just because an amazing man had captured her attention? "Besides," she continued, wanting to make sure this door was good and closed and she could move on. That had been some kiss and would require some serious damage control to move past, though. "We both have other things to focus on. Definitely we don't need to get distracted, or..."

He nodded. "Yeah, distracted."

It felt like they were both doing the same thing, piling on excuses, as though the current between them could be broken if only they verbalized enough reasons to set their feelings aside.

Whatever the reason, Finn did not want to kiss her again, did not want to be in any kind of relationship with her.

And Jordyn was probably better off alone anyway. Like she'd thought earlier, she should be used to it by now.

"So, um..." She cleared her throat. "You were saying we should go search the creek."

"Yeah, but if you don't think it's a good idea."

"No, I do. I definitely do." She hadn't meant for her words to have any kind of undertone, but *I do* wasn't the best choice in that case. Hopefully Finn wouldn't notice. "I think it's a great idea. If there's any hope of finding something about her case that isn't cold, we're going to have to get searching and find a new lead. Nothing's going to just fall in our laps."

She offered a smile that she hoped was encouraging as she started the car again. Because it *was* a good idea. And also because she wanted to have something to do, anything to distract her from the full realization of the feelings she was developing for a man she'd never be able to have.

# FIFTEEN

Finn thought he saw a shadow flicker over her face and could only guess at what she was thinking as she drove to Canyon Creek. If it was about the kiss…

He didn't want to worry about that right now; they'd said all that could be said on the subject. They'd just have to wait and see how things turned out. She'd blamed herself, but Finn knew it was his fault. He'd let his attraction to her get the best of his good sense. They couldn't be together. Jordyn had made that clear when she'd all but said the kiss shouldn't have happened since they couldn't get distracted. He had to respect that. And maybe he should admit he'd closed off his heart for too long and probably wasn't capable of being in a functional relationship. It scared him more than several standoffs he'd been involved in, the idea of starting a relationship with Jordyn, but he might just be ready to face that fear… Jordyn… Jordyn didn't seem like she was. She wasn't interested in a relationship. And Finn didn't like to start things he couldn't finish.

"I'll get Cipher," she finally said after parking the car at the trailhead. She exited and got the dog out of the back. Cipher, still in her vest, looked ready to go to work. She looked prepared for the search, eager.

Jordyn… Jordyn looked weary. Beautiful, but exhausted.

"You okay?" he asked after stepping out of the car.

"I'm fine."

"I didn't mean to push you into this," he started, glancing over at her, wishing he could take a moment and see her face better. But in investigations like this, he couldn't shake the idea that every moment counted. Every hour and day that passed without another victim disappearing was something to be thankful for, but it was also an indication that the next attack was coming, that someone would die soon if he didn't do anything to stop it.

She offered him a half smile, and for maybe the first time, he saw how much this cost her. She'd told him once that with search dogs, and specifically cadaver dogs, you had to be careful to balance their life with rewards for doing their job. Otherwise the knowledge that the people they were finding were dead would wear on them, actually depress the dog. Now he realized that the same was true of the handlers for these dogs.

Their complicated attraction aside, this investigation was hard for Jordyn. He understood that.

They started the search, leaving the parking lot and heading into the woods. "I didn't think about what this was costing you," he said after a moment.

The silence between them this time wasn't stretched or tense or awkward. It was full. Heavy. But in a way that was settling rather than oppressive. Her eyes were shining.

"I'm sorry," he found himself saying. "I'm sorry I didn't think about how much chasing down every single lead today must be hard for you."

She wiped her eyes with a hand, the motion rushed and frustrated. "It's not like it's easy for you."

"Yeah, but you do this all the time. Looking for people's

bodies." He saw plenty of grittiness in his job, but she was in the grittiness all the time.

More silence.

Jordyn blew out a breath. "Thanks. For seeing it. For seeing me."

This time, the stillness was full in a different way. Somehow they felt closer right now than they had when they kissed. Thanks for seeing her? Was that what he was doing?

But wasn't that what they were both doing? Scenes from the past week flashed through his mind. Laughing with her. Talking about the case. About Tori. Running for their lives. He'd never once felt like he was having to hide who he really was, or to put on any kind of face for her.

She saw him too.

It was jarring, this realization that even if they had tried to back off after that kiss, they were still so close to each other. How was he supposed to leave Alaska now? Could he, even? Did he want to?

It was the place where so many of his worst memories had been, but so many of his best too. And he felt less… finished with his life here in Alaska than he'd felt before. Before he'd been attacked, reunited with Jordyn, gotten to know her. It had seemed like everything about Alaska was a chapter he was ready to leave behind.

But now? He didn't know. He couldn't be sure what the future would hold, other than that he couldn't currently imagine a future without her in it.

She was still looking at him, he realized. Waiting for a response to her thanks. "You're welcome," he finally said, looking away. He cleared his throat.

His heart was pounding but in a different way than it ever had in relation to this case, through all the fear he'd felt when investigating it. This was a different kind of fear.

Of how close he felt to Jordyn. Of what would change if he left Alaska. And what would change if he didn't.

His phone rang. "Hello?"

"We need you at the Eagle Bend PD," Agent Littleton's words were tense.

"Details?"

"I can't give them to you over the phone, but it's important. The killer finally left a trail. Get here immediately."

Emotions warred within him, and he wanted to yell with frustration but blew out a long breath instead.

"Bad news?" she asked in that way of hers that didn't make him feel pressured to talk, but somehow always seemed to make it clear that he could talk if he wanted to.

"Good news, technically. The FBI has a break in the case. Apparently the killer left some kind of trail."

"After all this time?" Jordyn's voice was doubtful.

"I know. Believe me, I don't..." He ran a hand through his hair, batting away all the things he really wanted to say. What, that he didn't want to leave her? That he'd been hoping beyond hope that today might be the day they had a break in Tori's case and found some kind of closure? He'd probably been foolish investigating her case alongside this current one, but no matter how much the FBI party line seemed to push back on that, he was convinced they were linked. "I would rather search with you guys," he finally said.

"But you've got a job to do."

The way she said it did something to him that made him put his shoulders back and push away any lingering doubts. She was right.

He could almost imagine Tori laughing if she were here, at his realization that he needed her friend's wisdom. He'd always had a feeling Jordyn was smart and someone worth knowing. He just hadn't had any idea how right he was.

"Yeah. I do," he finally said aloud, blowing out another breath. "I'll take you to your house. Stay there until I come back. We are too close to take any risks." In addition to the information they'd found out, he could feel something happening in his mind too, like when you're close to the answer of a puzzle, or you're close to remembering something you've wanted to say and forgotten. When he thought about the attack now, there wasn't just blackness and blankness in his mind. There was static. The sense that if he just relaxed and didn't try to force the memories, they were so close to returning.

He said nothing about that to Jordyn, though, not wanting to get her hopes up in case he was wrong. They'd be better off counting on what they could quantify, like searching where they'd planned to search today. This was just a delay. They could wait.

"I don't want to go back," Jordyn spoke up, looking away from Cipher just long enough to meet his eyes. "Cipher's making real progress here, I can tell."

"It's not safe."

"Nowhere is, in case you've forgotten. If I go back home, the killer could still find me there. I don't want to be a sitting duck, Finn. I don't want to be a victim. If the killer finds me, I want to know I was fighting back and doing what I could to finally figure out who they are."

"Sorry, Jordyn." He was already shaking his head. "I don't think it's a good idea."

A rustle in the brush startled him, and Finn glanced to his right, where the noise had been, and was just in time to see Cipher disappearing into the brush.

"See?" Jordyn's eyes were practically sparkling with excitement. "She's got something."

He stood still, pulled in two directions. Either decision felt wrong.

"Go do your job," she said with enough confidence that he almost believed he could do it. "I've got to go catch my dog."

He hesitated. "At least text Sergeant Patrick. Let him know you need backup the second you know where Cipher is and where you might be headed. Surely they don't need everyone down there."

"I'll do that. Go, Finn. I'll be fine."

Jordyn hurried down the Canyon Falls Creek trail after Cipher, out of breath, mind spinning with excitement and nerves as she tried to notice all the details she could, tried not to get too far behind Cipher and tried to think about Tori's case. This place felt far from Tori's point last seen, since both trailheads were on opposite sides of town, but when they'd looked at the map earlier today and seen again how close they actually were, and considered all they'd learned, it seemed reasonable enough to do another search.

Jordyn hadn't been able to help with the initial search at the Canyon Falls Creek trail. The Eagle Bend Police Department was small enough that they'd welcomed community involvement in the ground searches, so Jordyn had been able to help a bit even though she didn't have any experience. It was what she'd done whenever she wasn't watching the K-9 teams in fascination. The bottom of the creek was laden with boulders and because of that was extremely dangerous. Even thrill seekers avoided Canyon Falls Creek for rafting, for the most part. A couple of people were rescued or died every few years, determined to attempt what others had deemed unsafe.

Hopefully Cipher wasn't down there.

Realistically, she wouldn't be able to search the bottom of the falls. She didn't have the equipment to safely get down there. It would have to be enough for her to know that the bottom had been searched thoroughly five years ago. Today she'd focus on the top. Unless Cipher didn't turn up.

She wasn't used to wrestling with this feeling of aloneness, this feeling of…fear?

Was that it? Was she afraid?

Jordyn was used to feeling uncomfortable during searches, and during the things she did for fun. It was Alaska. Half of their leisure activities were routinely on risk-assessment lists to represent dangerous activities. But this felt different somehow, and for a minute she almost didn't continue.

Then she thought of Tori and all the questions she had that continued to go unanswered. She was tired of not knowing.

And besides, there was no way she was leaving her dog.

She'd promised Finn she'd text her boss. Maybe she should do that now, even though she didn't know for sure where Cipher was, wasn't quite clear on exactly where the dog might lead her once she had found her. If she found her. The uneasy feeling in her stomach churned even harder.

Could she trust her boss? She thought so. But the wrong move would spell certain death out here in such an isolated location.

She decided it was a risk she had to take.

Moving quickly, she tapped out a message to Sergeant Patrick.

Going to search near Canyon Falls Creek. If you don't hear from me by six p.m. send help. Don't tell anyone you don't trust. I'll explain later.

It was hours away, more than enough time to search the trail, more than enough time to run into trouble and not be able to get herself out, but at least someone else knew where she was now. Hopefully she'd not just alerted a killer to her movements.

She glanced up from her phone, saw Cipher standing, panting, like she'd realized she'd lost her handler and waited.

"Good girl." She reached out, petted her behind the ears. It wasn't enough. Jordyn bent down, wrapped her arms around her dog's chest and back and buried her face in her fur, breathing in her familiar scent.

She was okay. They were both going to be okay.

"Cipher, search."

And they took off together down the trail.

# SIXTEEN

The second Finn had felt his phone buzz at the police station, he'd known what the message would be. Jordyn was searching anyway, even though he was stuck here at the police department and she was there, alone with Cipher, with a killer still on the loose.

Being back in the police department on official business was strange. He could remember working here, and the edges of his mind felt looser, like even more of his memory from the past week was returning. He remembered the bullpen here, how they'd do roll call with the other guys from the department then meet specifically with those involved in this investigation to go over the case.

He made his way to the conference room, where all of the officers, agents and other auxiliary employees who had been working on the case were gathered.

"Looks like we finally have some resolution," Sergeant Patrick said by way of greeting. "Anchorage Police Department just called and talked to someone from the Bureau."

He went on to explain the details of the call. The information they'd brought him in to show him had been important, and Finn understood the urgency now. They were about to close the case. Patrick was confident that they'd found their killer in Kurt Olsen, a man from Anchorage who had been tied to a murder there this past weekend. A woman who was of a similar age to the women who'd been targeted in Eagle Bend had been found dead, shot point-blank in the forehead, on the Ship Creek trail there and police had forwarded his name to the FBI for consideration in this case. So far, it looked fairly obvious. Open and shut.

They were assembling a team to make the arrest, most of them being pulled in to play different roles and make sure it went as smoothly as possible. It was all hands on deck—but Finn's injury gave him a good reason to ask to sit it out. Theoretically he was going home to rest.

Really, he was hurrying to find Jordyn. He sped to his car, discomfort building in him.

It was his worst fears for this case coming true. Maybe not worst fears—those involved Jordyn being physically harmed. But high up there on the list was Tori's case going cold again, when he was convinced there was a connection that others just hadn't seen yet or weren't willing to see. He didn't think Kurt could be the one behind the rash of murders. His gut instinct, his fragmented memories, said it was someone at the FBI. Or connected to the FBI, maybe an Eagle Bend police officer. He knew the killer; he was sure of it.

This was the reason he couldn't be upset with Jordyn for going to search without him. Every minute counted.

Knowing all of that didn't make it any easier to think of her out there alone, though, especially on the Canyon Falls Creek trail. It was just as isolated as where they'd been concentrating their search efforts, but the terrain was even more rugged and dangerous. He knew Cipher and Jordyn were both capable, but there were still so many ways a person could get into trouble in the Alaskan wilderness, not the least of which was to draw the attention of a serial killer to themselves.

Which was exactly what Jordyn was doing if this new theory was *not* correct and the killer wasn't this guy in Anchorage who'd murdered the woman there. If he *wasn't* the killer, then him going to jail for all of these crimes would set another killer free. Possibly the one who had murdered Tori, if his thoughts were correct, but either way, the person truly responsible for these crimes would go free unless they found something to prove that Kurt Olsen from Anchorage had not been responsible.

Jordyn, he realized with gut-stabbing clarity, was in more danger now than she'd been during this entire investigation.

The drive to the trailhead took forever, every second feeling like a minute or more. He had no way of knowing which way she'd searched, and even though cell phones theoretically could send text messages in the backcountry with this latest iPhone update, real-world experience said that couldn't always be counted on. Jordyn was out of sight, out of reach and entirely out of his control.

The thought needled him, but it was more than that, he realized as he pulled on a rain jacket just in case the weather turned bad, locked his car and jogged away from it. It was the issue of control entirely. God was supposed to be in control, *was* in control according to everything Finn had ever been taught, but if that was true, really true, how did someone explain all the bad things that happened in the world? He knew it wasn't an original problem to have with the concept of God's sovereignty, but he couldn't wrap his mind around it.

Now probably wasn't the time to try, he decided, as the trail narrowed the closer he got to the ravine and the creek.

Canyon Creek consisted of several trails that led various places, but he and Jordyn had both felt strongly that the boulders near the creek were a promising place to look for evidence. Or, to be honest, Tori's remains.

If her remains were in some as yet unsearched location, it would be one that was difficult to reach. There were several places along the trail that might fit that description, and their plan had been for Jordyn to bring Cipher to those and see what she smelled. Depending on several different factors, Cipher might be able to find something by scent, something Finn found remarkable. It was likely that Jordyn was sticking to their plan, and that meant that wherever she was, it would likely be at least somewhat difficult to access. In a way that made her safer, since someone who wanted to hurt her would have to get to her first, but if the wrong person did find her, exiting wouldn't be easy. It also made it more difficult for Finn to find her.

He didn't have the benefit of a K-9, but he did have the tracking skills he'd learned through his FBI training, so it shouldn't be impossible. The only questions were how long would it take—and would he be too late?

It was so like the thought he'd had several days ago… He stumbled and had to catch himself. He remembered. He remembered that day, the morning of the attack. He'd come up the trail toward the clearing, the one where Cipher and Jordyn had found him, and he'd wondered if he was too late. He'd gotten some kind of intel…

Someone had seen the most recently murdered woman with someone he knew, and he'd wanted to find out how they knew each other. That was it. He'd left the coffee shop, driven to the trailhead, hiked to the clearing…

*It's you…* He could hear himself saying the words out

loud, his voice stunned. He could feel how he'd felt then. Disgusted. Afraid. Surprised.

But when he probed his mind, he still couldn't see the face, still didn't know who it was.

He was only entirely certain now that he knew who it was. If he could control his mind, harness it somehow...

This wasn't something he could try harder at and make work, though. He was entirely incapable of strong-arming his memory into recalling what he wanted to know.

He'd spent so many years pushing his faith away, telling God all the reasons he wasn't sure he believed in him anymore, but that still, small voice took him by surprise. He heard it, felt it, an awareness of God reminding him that he, Finn, was never in control. Not really. God was.

God was in control?

The whisper of certainty in his heart transformed into a question as he turned it over and over and tried to decide if he believed it, when suddenly it became a certainty again. What did it matter if he believed it? He was so small—if that wasn't obvious in the Alaskan wilderness, he didn't know where it would be. The entire landscape dwarfed him—one small human in this vastness that was still just a corner of the state, a small part of the entire world, over which God was in control.

*Was*. That was a fact—which he'd always been taught was true and had believed until the time that his sister didn't come home—whether he believed it or not. God had been in control when Tori disappeared. And He was in control now. Suddenly that was clearer than anything else, clearer than the things he could see with his own eyes.

*Help, God.* He prayed, believing fully that God would. Later, there would be time to talk to Him more, to dive into the details of his struggles and ask God to heal him in the ways he needed to be healed, but right now, he just knew he needed Him, that he needed God to uncover the missing details in his mind, help him find Jordyn and keep them both safe.

And he needed all of those things fast.

The darkness between the spruce trees was at once intoxicating, lovely and terrifying. With every step she took, Jordyn knew she was moving toward something; she could feel it. This wouldn't be another dead end. Their hunch, at least to some degree, was right; she was sure of it. The question was, how many answers would she get today?

And how many did she need?

The trail became more technical this far into the woods, as she was searching on a line that would take her and Cipher as close to the bottom of the canyon as it was possible to get without technical rock-climbing gear. She was fairly certain the entire canyon had been searched by teams with ropes and harnesses, at least at the bottom by the creek. But some of the little indentations in the rock and corner trails that were isolated and difficult to get to could have been overlooked. This was where their information had led them, at least in her opinion. Jordyn found herself wishing she and Finn had discussed in more detail where they were going to search, because when he was done with that meeting, she wanted him here with her.

The closer they got to river, the more Cipher was giving clues that something was catching her attention. She was no longer trotting along with her mouth open and panting; she'd closed it, and she was visibly sniffing in the air in a way that was direct enough Jordyn could almost imagine that she could see the scent cones. Because of that, Jordyn wound them closer, walking on some edges of the trail that were high enough she had to force herself not to look down in order to make herself go farther. She wouldn't say she had a fear of heights, but she had a healthy respect for them anyway. Cipher was surefooted and able to navigate the terrain without difficulty, or Jordyn wouldn't have attempted to come this way.

Her foot slipped and Jordyn had to reach out and grab a spruce tree, taking a minute to calm her breathing and bring her heart rate back down. It was entirely impractical because she knew Finn was too far away to help right now, but when she'd safely moved to a wider area, she pulled out her phone and checked for a response from Finn. Nothing. He had to have seen the text, at least she thought so. She'd sent it from the parking lot, and she knew she had service there.

I'm near the river, back on one of those trails that has a lot of dead ends.

It wasn't much to go on, but if it went through, at least it would help…

Not even ten seconds passed before the Message Failed to Send notification popped up. So much for hoping they'd be able to communicate. She and her husky were truly alone.

How much did time matter right now? She felt like this was urgent, like if they went back to the trailhead to wait for Finn they'd lose valuable time. Would it really hurt to wait, though, and be extra safe? The danger she faced was real, tangible. On the other hand, what if Cipher lost the scent when they left? Air-scent searches were extremely variable. Scent pockets could change based on wind and a number of other factors.

She couldn't risk the search. She'd just have to do it feeling alone.

It was a feeling she should be familiar with by now, she told herself as she kept following Cipher into the growing darkness of the dark forest. She'd been alone in a lot of ways since Tori had died. New friends had seemed too hard to make, a boyfriend impossible, not when she wasn't willing to get close to anyone. And how could she do that? People *left*. Sometimes, like with Tori, they didn't want to, but it didn't change how much it hurt when they did. Going through that again, for any reason, felt like too much to ask of herself.

That was why this thing with Finn was a mistake. She shouldn't have let him get so close, because no matter what she'd told herself earlier, somewhere inside she knew the truth, that he was going to leave like he'd always planned.

Grief felt heavy on her, and while she wanted to tell herself that the physical darkness wasn't helping, Jordyn knew it was affecting her mood and attitude. She needed to find Tori's body if it was out here. They needed closure. Until they had it, grief would be an unwanted shadow that weighed down even moments that should be innocuous.

It was just something that was true.

Up ahead, sunlight sliced through the tall trees and shone down into the ravine. It was so unexpected, such a contrast to the darkness, that it caught her attention, even before Cipher sprinted toward it. Jordyn followed her, hurrying toward the light.

What if…what if Tori wasn't here? What if they never found her?

They were thoughts she'd had before, though she'd tried hard not to let herself think them. Now, here in the woods with only Cipher for company, she made herself face them.

They might never have closure. Was that okay?

It had to be. It wasn't like she had a choice. She should stuff these feelings, get back on the trail she'd meant to search, not this side trail, and move on again. She'd done that plenty of times.

"What if, God? What if I don't find her?" she whispered, calling Cipher to her and moving back toward the trail she'd been on earlier. How was she supposed to be okay if this never resolved, if she could never move on?

Grief never went away, she knew that. She'd certainly talked to enough people in the wake of the events of five years ago who had wanted to help. She'd read books. If this was something she could have DIYed, she'd have been able to move on, move past it, however you wanted to say it, a long time ago.

What if that wasn't the point? What if she never found her friend? What if she had to move on anyway, trust that God's justice was perfect and that He knew what He was doing even if it never made any sense to her?

When she asked the question, it settled on her like a reassuring weight. God had to be enough. *Was* enough. Not answers. Not guidance. He wasn't some kind of force she was supposed to just seek when she wanted to know something or wanted her life to have all of its loose ends tied. In fact, maybe that was the opposite of what she actually needed.

Jordyn inhaled deeply, the air moist with the cold water from the falls in the canyon below blowing toward them. She felt…the same. Except entirely different. Like maybe this would really be the time when it would make sense to her, when she'd be able to trust that God had a plan, that He was enough.

And maybe it was. And maybe she'd have to come to Him again tomorrow, surrendering the same things she'd tried to let go of today, but somehow this time, that was okay. She knew it was, with full confidence.

"Thank you," she whispered to Him aloud. Then took another breath to re-center her focus on where she was, what she was doing.

The moisture in the air was the first thing that caught her attention, and it brought her back to the present. Jordyn hadn't realized how close to the falls she was. She'd gone deeper into the woods than she'd realized. Cipher hadn't gone quite back the way they'd come when Jordyn had taken her detour. Instead she'd moved down another small side trail, this one a narrow switchback that led toward the moisture in the air and the dim roaring sound of the waterfall. Careful of her footing, Jordyn followed Cipher. But Cipher didn't head down the trail to the falls. Not exactly. She was nearby, but not on the official trail, Jordyn thought. Cipher was out of Jordyn's vision now and something like panic gripped at Jordyn. Jordyn didn't think her dog had gone down the falls trail. She could still see those switchbacks. There were no other trails, though. Just brush and plants...

There. Hidden among a tall plant with purple stems and tiny white flowers was another trail. Narrow.

Was that where Cipher had gone? Jordyn backed up a couple of steps, where she had a better view of the surrounding area. She didn't see the husky anywhere. It had only been a couple of seconds that Jordyn had looked away when Cipher could have disappeared. She had to have gone this way.

Pushing aside the flowers, Jordyn moved forward, finally catching a glimpse of Cipher's tail, relief flooding her. Jordyn emerged from the brush just in time to see Cipher's face jerk as she distinctly caught a scent. She kept moving forward, all focus now. They were somewhere near the bottom of the ravine, but Jordyn couldn't quite sort out where they were in relation to the waterfall. Possibly they were winding behind it? There were boulders they were weaving through now, and it reminded her of the boulder field in a way that made her have to take deep breaths to relieve tension. The boulders were tall and stretched well above her head, some smooth, most rough and jagged on the edges. Some were damp.

Ahead, behind the boulders, the creek formed a small pool at the base of what wasn't quite a cave, but was more of a rocky outcropping.

Jordyn had never known this was here, had never gone off the main trail. Judging by how overgrown it was back here, she doubted many people knew of this place. She'd search quickly, since Cipher seemed insistent on it, then go back to where there was service and try to call Finn. She didn't want to be back here alone for long. She felt like she and Cipher were the only living beings on the face of the earth.

But not the only beings...

Cipher had laid down beside the edge of the overhang. She let out a low, desperate bay.

Behind her, Jordyn could see the off-white color of bones. She swallowed hard. This was what she'd been looking for, but she hadn't been ready to find it, not really. Here they were anyway, she could tell by the metal ankle bracelet around the leg bone near the foot. Tori's remains.

# SEVENTEEN

If she tried for years, decades, a lifetime, Jordyn knew she would never be able to reconcile the bones with Tori as Jordyn remembered her. Laughing, bossy, ponytail swinging. For the first time, that word that had come to mind, *remains*, really struck her. It was all that was left physically, and an apt description because of that. But now it called to her mind the fact that Tori wasn't here. Her spiritual self had not remained here, her essence had not died when her body did, it was alive even now in Heaven. This was just… what was left. The remains.

It made the scene easier to process, and Jordyn was able to take a deep breath and move toward the bones. She avoided the middle of the pool, keeping to the drier rocks on the outer edges, toward the back of the outcropping where the bones were.

"Cipher, come. Good girl." The dog moved toward Jordyn without hesitation, and Jordyn scratched her neck and behind her ears, trying to ease some of the dog's visible tension. After giving her a couple of treats from her pocket, she moved toward the bones.

She was no crime scene investigator, not law enforcement of any kind, but she knew they had tests that would be able to confirm that the bones were Tori's in a way that was much more official than the visual confirmation that the ankle bracelet had given her. Once they'd done that, what else would these bones be able to tell them? For years this had been her hope, once she'd realized Tori wasn't coming home alive, that at least they'd be able to find whatever was left of her, bury her properly, let the past finally lie in peace. But what else? Could these bones hold any kind of clue to who had been behind her death? Would they really, as she and Finn had hoped, hold some kind of key that would finally bring this to an end?

She understood it now, what people said in all those cheesy sports movies about how if you aren't enough *without* whatever it is you're chasing, you won't be enough with it. If she hadn't realized that God was in control whether they ever found Tori's remains or not, this moment still wouldn't be enough because there were still unanswered questions, still the unresolved tension of a death that had come too soon.

The skeleton appeared to her untrained eye to be in one piece, as though Tori's body had been tucked into the narrow space between the rocks on the ground and the outcropping formed by the large boulders and rocky cliffside of the canyon. It was a brilliant hiding place. The scent was trapped, only accessible on one of the sides, the breeze and moisture from the waterfall serving both to confuse search dogs as well as speed up decomposition. When Jordyn first started considering getting a human remains dog, she'd done a lot of research into that process and was aware of the basics of how long it took a body to become a skeleton in various conditions. This location was ideal for a murderer to hide a body until there wasn't much left of it.

If she and Cipher hadn't taken that trail to see the sun, they might not have ended up in a place where her dog could have caught the scent. What had seemed like a coincidence to Jordyn, a side trail, had turned out to be necessary.

Knowing her odds weren't likely to be any better getting service down here, she pulled out her phone to send a text to Finn anyway. Just in case.

"Well. Look at that. You finally found her."

A low female voice spoke above the din of the falls, its words smooth. The tone soothing, despite the menacing words.

The click of the hammer of a revolver being dropped.

Cipher growled and Jordyn whipped around, heart sinking as she realized what she was going to see, and then saw it for herself. Melissa Reynolds, standing backlit in the entrance to the cave.

The profiler looked like she always did, Jordyn noted without really meaning to, her eyes taking in all the details, slowing time down as some kind of defense mechanism. Not a hair was out of place, and she wore a nice shirt, pressed trousers and thoroughly impractical shoes.

Holding a revolver toward Jordyn.

"Poetic, isn't it? That you're going to die right where she did."

Jordyn's breath caught in her throat. Most of the women they'd found so far had been killed somewhere other than their final resting place.

"I'd planned to move her," Melissa answered Jordyn's question before she could even ask it. "But the search started too quickly. Much more quickly than I anticipated, and I didn't have a good plan for confusing the search. I learned a lot that first time." The side of her mouth quirked in a sick smile.

"The first time?" Jordyn asked, deciding that playing dumb might work better than telling Melissa everything they knew or suspected. After all, she was already being held at gunpoint by a woman she knew had killed before. It hardly seemed that the situation could get much worse.

Unfortunately, Melissa was too good at her day job. "Don't pretend you have no idea. You knew your friend here—" she gestured toward Tori's bones with the gun "—was the first I killed. I killed the other women also."

While as much had been implied, her blatant admission of guilt sent cold chills down Jordyn's spine. This woman had murdered her best friend. The weight of it hit her in the chest like a punch. Anger. Sadness too deep to explain. She felt gutted. And yet, not weakened. The admission of guilt had strengthened her resolve to see Melissa brought to justice. She would not give up now. Besides, if there had been any doubt that Melissa wasn't going to let her out of here alive, there wasn't now. There was no caution in the way she was talking. Jordyn wasn't even sure there was calculation. Committing murder required, to Jordyn's point of view, some breakdown of the normal human mind, to be able to justify the unjustifiable. But Melissa's mind had taken another leap, it seemed. While she looked the same, her voice sounded the same—so deeply calming even as she said horrible things, probably a side effect of her job as a psychologist—something was slightly off. Her eyes were a little wider. She was jumpy. Unhinged.

"Why such a long break between Tori and the others. Five years?"

She shrugged. "I left the state. Tori's killing went so well."

Jordyn wanted to throw up.

"Oh please." Melissa rolled her eyes. "Save the dramatics. I've had enough drama for twenty careers. People and their emotions disgust me."

"Aren't you supposed to sort through people's emotions and motivations, like…wasn't that the whole point of your career?"

Another eye roll. "Learn how to manipulate them, sure. That was what was so interesting about these murders. It was a social experiment, really. How many women had to disappear before a town became paranoid and assumed there was a serial killer behind every tree? How easy was it to lure women away from the safety of their workplaces, hiking trails, parking lots? Could I really commit a murder and get away with it? And if I could commit one, could I commit more?"

She was psychotic. Entirely broken. Jordyn could see now the hollowness in her eyes, the hopelessness etched on every line of her face. Melissa may feel in control, but she'd given herself over to this sickness and made herself a slave to evil.

And maybe Jordyn should feel sorry for her, but she did not. Melissa had made her choices. She only felt a deep sense of sadness, heaviness, for all of those affected. For the women who had been killed recently. For Tori. The families. Finn. Herself. Everyone who had been a victim or been connected to one.

Thoughts swirled in her mind as she processed what Melissa had said, thought about her own struggles to be in charge. People like Melissa thought they were unbreakable. Everything Melissa was saying made sense to her; it was all justified, but it wasn't. The woman wasn't an idiot; she knew she'd done things wrong. Jordyn hadn't gotten very far in her psychology degree, but she'd had enough intro classes that she thought…maybe…

Could she outthink her? Do some manipulating of her own to save herself? Because much as it sounded appealing to wait for Finn to come save her, kiss him senseless with relief and then ride off into the sunset together, Jordyn had a feeling that wasn't an outcome she could count on.

"And did you really think you were going to get away with it?" Jordyn asked slowly as she turned her idea over in her mind. Did she know enough about people to pull this off? Did she understand Melissa?

Jordyn knew she did not and never would understand the other woman's disgusting motivations for committing such evil. But as far as the way her mind worked...could she figure out what would make her feel in control and somehow give it to her, feed it to her in such a way that she kept talking, let Jordyn live longer, gave her a way to escape?

"I was always sure I would." Her eyes shone. "Except for Jenna Matthews."

Jenna Matthews. Finn had mentioned her on their drive the other day, not connected to the case, really, but vaguely connected to Tori's murder somehow? Jordyn racked her brain. Jenna...that was right, she'd disappeared right after Tori and the public had assumed there was a serial killer, but then she'd returned to her parents' house safely and with a satisfactory explanation, and the case had gone cold. The family had been fairly new in Eagle Bend when Jenna disappeared, and then Jenna had left, probably for college, soon after. Jordyn didn't remember seeing her around town since then.

Had she helped cover up Tori's disappearance somehow? Almost been a victim herself? Or had her case been entirely unconnected?

Jordyn knew that the last time she'd asked questions it hadn't gone well, but she truly didn't know enough about Jenna Matthews to make the connection here. She took the chance of asking again.

"Jenna Matthews?" she asked.

Melissa, who had been looking into the distance, though still holding the gun barrel in Jordyn's direction, looked back at her, eyes sharp. Her expression softened.

"You really didn't figure it out? Maybe I could have gotten away with that one too..." She trailed off.

"Tell me about her," Jordyn said and wondered if Melissa would answer, or if she'd grow tired of the way she was drawing this out and just shoot her. She stared down the barrel of the gun, willing herself to stay calm, to breathe slowly.

And waited.

The switchbacks that led down toward the bottom of the ravine had a myriad of side trails, made mostly by moose and bears, Finn would guess. This certainly wasn't somewhere people came often, though Alaskans were known for exploring absolutely anywhere they could reasonably access as well as places that took a large amount of effort to get to.

He chose the trail that led to the front of the waterfall, hoping against hope that Jordyn hadn't really come this way. The trail was slick, and every time he placed his foot down, he had to test it to see if he would be able to keep his balance on the steep grade and mud.

A slight noise behind him made him tense, but when he looked behind him, he saw nothing. Only trees, weeds, wilderness.

Then he heard the voice.

"Freeze."

He didn't know how he hadn't seen her, except that she'd concealed herself in the brush well. It was Officer Lee from the Eagle Bend Police Department. She was still dressed head to toe in police gear and her dark hair was in a low ponytail. Her expression was serious, but not as serious as the Glock 17 she was pointing at him.

Officer Lee?

He replayed the scene in his mind that he'd been struggling to remember.

*It's you.*

This time he heard more in his recollection.

*Yes, it's me.* And the voice he remembered hearing was female.

Fear hit him for a moment, and nausea rose in his throat…

But the voice in his memory wasn't Officer Lee's. Was his memory faulty? If she wasn't the person who had attacked him, why was she standing here holding a gun and pointing it at him?

"What are you doing?" he asked.

"That's a question I should be asking you." Her eyes narrowed. "Don't think I didn't see through that story. I've spent too many years studying behavior and working in this job not to notice that you and Jordyn didn't just happen to meet up. There's more to this. What's the whole story here? And before you feed me some kind of crap, you should know that I know this case inside and out and I have a personal investment in it being solved. Are you involved somehow?"

"In solving it, yes."

"With *her*? Are you helping *her*? She vouched for you earlier."

"Who, Jordyn?"

Officer Lee was already shaking her head. "Melissa Reynolds."

The impact of her words hit him harder than a bullet.

Melissa Reynolds, the profiler? The starchy, calm, clean psychologist?

But it fit.

Eyebrows pressing together in a confused frown, Lee started to lower the weapon, as if his face was telling her everything she needed to know—that he was innocent.

"Why are you out here?" he asked.

"My boss got a text from Jordyn. I didn't like how it sounded. I've watched enough women disappear in these woods." The words were bitter. Deeply personal, and once again Finn was struck by how seriously she took this case.

"I have too. One of them was my sister."

She nodded slowly. "I know…" Then she trailed off. "And one of them was me."

His eyebrows shot up, but he studied her face under the tactical baseball cap she always wore low over her face with a police uniform. Her face, largely shadowed by the cap, reminded him of something he'd seen in the files the other day…or had it only been yesterday?…when he'd been looking at Tori's case. The missing woman who hadn't been missing. Green eyes. Heart-shaped face and delicate features. But her hair was dark. Jenna's had been light. "Jenna Matthews. But…your hair…and…" His eyes flickered to her name badge. Lee.

"I dyed my hair. Started working out so I wouldn't ever be caught in such a vulnerable position again. It obscuring my identity was a side benefit. Lee is my stepdad's name. I took his name after I left town, not wanting to be connected to that part of my past. My family moved to Eagle Bend when I was already in college. I came with them, thinking maybe this would be a cool town to live in." She shook her head. "And I almost ended up like every single one of them." She met his eyes. "Like Jordyn is going to if we don't find her soon. You really don't know where she is?" Her eyes narrowed again.

"If I knew where she was, I would be there, making sure she was safe."

Jenna's eyes widened, like she heard what he felt, what he'd heard in his own tone, though it remained unspoken.

He didn't know where she was. But he did love her.

"Wait, you two…" She trailed off. "Does she know? How you feel, I mean?"

"Maybe. I'm not sure." He rubbed his head, which was starting to hurt. Residual pain from the concussion, he guessed. Those didn't exactly heal overnight, or even over the space of a week.

"So how did you get away? How did you know it was Melissa? Did you know this whole time?" Even though it would have been too late to save Tori, since she'd vanished before Jenna had mysteriously disappeared, it would gut him to know that six other women *had* died because Jenna kept her mouth shut, but she was already shaking her head.

"Not until recently. And I only had my suspicions. That's why I haven't come forward with anything. I'm law enforcement, just like you are. I know the laws. I didn't have enough. And I didn't know who to trust."

Well, he understood that.

"I'll answer the rest of your questions later, but we have to find Jordyn." Her voice was urgent. "When her text came in to Sergeant Patrick and he told me about it, I looked around for Melissa immediately, but she'd already left. I don't know if she's got ears somewhere else and is working with someone else, or if she's just good, or if she left the department earlier and was already following Jordyn. But when I couldn't confirm her location I knew Jordyn was in trouble if she was alone."

"Where should we go?" He was looking around even as he asked the question. "Wait, these plants, did you move through them?" There wasn't a trail there behind the bushes to their left, and maybe Jordyn had walked through there.

She shook her head, stepping past him to go ahead, realizing what he had, that the slight breaks in the stems of the wildflowers were from someone walking past them.

He could see Cipher's paw prints in the slick mud again, something he'd seen earlier on the trail but hadn't seen in a while. They'd disappeared into the brush at one point, and he'd assumed maybe they'd walked off the trail and were going to reconnect at some point. But maybe they'd taken another route entirely. He walked into the slightly damaged underbrush, noting when he could confirm signs that someone had walked this direction recently.

Jenna came up beside him and passed him, scanning the area. They were near the waterfall, he could hear it, but they weren't approaching it from the front. Finn had been in this ravine before. He'd rock climbed some in college and had had enough skills that during the search for Tori, he'd helped search not far from here. But he hadn't known this trail existed, wherever they were now. Behind the waterfall, maybe?

In front of him, Jenna stopped short.

"What?" he whispered.

"I hear voices. I think we're almost too late. But hopefully not." Her voice was clipped. Stressed. "Let's split up. You go around this way. I'm going to go in first, cause a distraction. Your job is to get that gun away from Melissa. She won't let anyone walk away if she can help it."

Finn nodded his agreement and moved forward. He was close enough now that he could hear Cipher's low growl.

"So I'm hiking with her, about to take her somewhere

and kill her, see if I can really can do this two times in a row, when suddenly she wants to go back" came Melissa's voice. She spoke the words so matter-of-factly, as if she wasn't describing a heinous crime. Finn's heart rate ratcheted up as he made his way toward the voice. "I tried to confuse her. We hiked in circles for hours. I thought I could still do it. It wasn't too late. I didn't have to find another victim, try again, I already had one… But she must have gotten suspicious. She started marking trees, called me out on the fact that we weren't making any progress. I knew at that point she'd see through any excuse I had, and I had to take us both back to town. I suppose I could have shot her, but part of the point was to do it in a way that was surprising. To not be suspected even by the victims."

Finn shuddered. Kept listening.

"Her parents had reported her missing already. Thankfully, she wasn't sure enough that something had been off—that I was actually up to anything suspicious—to report me. And why would she have? I was a successful psychology major who had just accepted a job with the FBI and was about to leave town, a stranger who had been nice enough to answer her post on social media asking for someone to hike with. What was she going to say, that I had gotten lost on an isolated hiking trail and accuse me of not having a sense of direction?" Melissa laughed and it was a hollow sound. "She told her parents she'd gotten confused hiking. Everyone went back to believing that Tori McDaniel's disappearance and assumed death had in fact been an isolated incident, not the first in a string of killings, like some had feared after Jenna disappeared. Maybe that's why people were so slow to panic when women started disappearing this time. And then it was too late…" Her voice trailed off.

Too late. Too late.

He'd been too late too many times. The muscles in Finn's body tensed.

"I'm going to shoot your dog now, so that she doesn't get in the way. And then, Jordyn, I'm going to shoot you. It's okay to be scared, you know. It's a common feeling." The last words were said with sarcasm. "But please, if you'd like to talk about it, don't. As I told you before, I am tired of hearing about people's emotions."

"Sounds like you should have picked another profession," a dry female voice broke in. Officer Lee.

Finn crept closer. He could see them now, in some kind of cave formed by several large boulders and the rock of the canyon wall. Jordyn was in the worst position, up against the rock, nowhere to escape. Melissa was between him and Jordyn. He had grabbed his service weapon, but he wouldn't be able to use it, not without risking unintentionally hitting Jordyn. His best option was to stick to the plan and disarm Melissa. If he moved too quickly and Melissa fired, there would be no coming back from that. One shot to the forehead. That was her MO. He would only have one chance to do this right.

Jordyn was counting on him. Jenna was counting on him. And while his sister was gone, in Heaven, and living a full life with God…somehow Finn felt like she was watching too, or maybe it was just the edges of her memory, reminding him that even though it was too late for her, it *was not* too late entirely.

He could still save someone. Hopefully several some-ones. Finn was determined.

# EIGHTEEN

"Sounds like you should have picked another profession." The voice came out of nowhere. Jordyn watched as Melissa jumped, and she felt herself tensing, expecting to be shot. Instead, Melissa swiveled and pointed her gun at the other woman who'd just walked up.

Officer Lee?

"Well, well. We were just talking about you," Melissa said, her voice sarcastic and cold. "Don't even think about pulling your weapon out or I'll shoot her right now."

"So you *did* recognize me." Officer Lee looked impressed, left the gun holstered.

Just talking about her… Recognize her…

"Wait." Jordyn thought about how Officer Lee had always seemed like she had more to her than met the eye. Her mind raced through what Melissa had just shared, about how she'd offered to hike with a woman who was new to town, intending to kill her, until it became obvious that this woman was suspicious. "You're Jenna Matthews?"

Officer Lee—Jenna—nodded. "I am. And it's about time someone brought this woman to justice." For the first time, Jenna seemed to notice the bones behind Jordyn. Her face softened a little. "Your friend?" she asked as she motioned toward them.

Jordyn nodded.

Relief was plain on Jenna's face. "That should be enough. There has to be enough evidence to convict her now."

"You've known?"

The other woman shook her head. "No. Only suspected. And only very recently. I've been watching her, trying to find something clear to tie her to the murders, but everything seemed circumstantial, and as a psychologist, she was a master at dropping hints here and there that made me feel like I was crazy for suspecting her at all." Jenna shook her head then turned to Reynolds. "Your head games are something."

"I should have shot you years ago." She raised the revolver, and Jordyn had no time to hesitate; she ran at Melissa, whose eyes widened as she swung the gun down on Jordyn's head. Jordyn jerked away, the revolver coming down on her head only as a glancing blow rather than the direct hit Jordyn suspected Finn had taken.

"No!" Finn's deep voice echoed nearby, and the distraction was just enough. Officer Lee shot at Melissa. A scream split the air.

Melissa's? Officer Lee's? Jordyn couldn't tell.

More shots rang out, these coming from Melissa. Toward Finn? Officer Lee? The space was too small to be able to tell, especially with the way the gunshot noise reverberated off of the boulders. She'd wanted to help, but Jordyn was caught in the crossfire now and stayed low.

She moved toward the boulder, farther from Melissa. If she could just get more space between them, would it be enough to give Finn a clear shot?

"You're not going anywhere," Melissa seethed.

Pain shot through her scalp as Melissa grabbed her by the hair and yanked her forward. Jordyn had no time to react before Melissa had pulled her in front of her. She was a human shield.

Jordyn hadn't had long to panic about her current predicament before it changed again and she felt herself being dragged toward the cave opening. She tried to kick, but Melissa was pulling her by the arms and hair, entirely undeterred by the way she fought back. As though she'd done this before.

"I think this is much more fitting, don't you? Your friend already has this cave. You need a new spot. Down by the creek maybe?"

Terror stole Jordyn's next breath, and she had to forcefully remind herself to breathe. The waterfall was treacherous, almost certain death if she couldn't stop Melissa before they got there. Finn and Officer Lee were going to try, she knew, but with Melissa holding her so tightly, it was going to be impossible to take her down without hurting Jordyn. At least, with a gun.

But not with a dog. Where was Cipher?

Jordyn looked back, took one final look at the boulder cave as Melissa yanked her out of it and noticed Finn holding Cipher's collar as he looked at her. She thought she could read the question in his eyes. Could Cipher do it?

Yes. She nodded slightly, wincing as the motion made Melissa yank her head harder the other way. Cipher could do it.

"You should never have stuck your nose where it didn't belong," Melissa said, voice calm again, apparently recentered by the events of the last few minutes. By her obvious regaining of control.

Except she didn't have control.

Cipher's growl was what Jordyn heard first, followed by a snarl, and then the impact of Cipher's body against

Melissa's. The profiler screamed, and by the long, agonizing sound of it, Cipher hadn't issued any kind of warning bite like she had during the break-in at Jordyn's house. This was a bite without bite inhibition, intended to harm.

Melissa dropped her weapon, which skidded several feet from where she'd stood, and fell to the ground, releasing her hold on Jordyn. Jordyn scrambled away, who took shelter back into the boulder cave. While the area was horrible to be in, with Tori's bones and the memories of the last few minutes, it was somewhat protected, and there would be boulders between her and Melissa, if the other woman recovered from the dog bite and came after her.

Finn and Officer Lee were already rushing through the opening, past Jordyn to where Melissa lay clutching her leg.

"We've got her!" Finn called back. Jordyn looked out, trying to breathe, trying to remember how, wrestling with how close she'd come to not being able to breathe again.

"You really caught me." Melissa blinked. "Five years. Seven women. Almost eight." She narrowed her eyes at Jenna then looked back at Jordyn. "And you caught me… with a stupid dog?"

Cipher almost looked like she was grinning. Jordyn rubbed her behind the ears. "Clearly not stupid."

She looked back at Finn. "I should have killed you when I had the chance. I had a gun. I should've shot you with it instead of hitting you over the head. But you weren't supposed to be there. You weren't supposed to mess up the scene. It wasn't how it was supposed to go."

Her sick need for order, for whatever disgusting logic she found in her crime scenes, had saved Finn's life.

"Do you remember? Being hit with the gun?" Jordyn looked to him and asked.

He nodded. "It all came back to me right before we found

you guys. I heard Officer Lee's voice and remembered the killer's voice was female, and it all fell back into place. I remember, Jordyn."

She briefly closed her eyes, a prayer of thanks in her heart. Finn wouldn't have lasting damage from the attack, hopefully. Regaining his memory was a good sign.

Noise from the pathway drew everyone's attention. Backup was arriving.

"Down here!" Jenna yelled up.

Sergeant Patrick entered, followed by Agent Hawkins and Agent Littleton. At seeing Melissa handcuffed, they looked to Jenna and Finn, who were both standing beside her. They both nodded toward Jordyn. "She should be the one to tell you. She's the one who found the proof," Jenna said and Finn nodded.

"She killed them," Jordyn said. "She killed them all, including Tori." She motioned to the bones behind her. "She confessed to killing them all verbally. And I suspect when you process the scene, you'll find that Tori was killed just like the others. She was going to kill Jenna here also…"

"Jen Lee… Jenna Matthews…" Sergeant Patrick blinked. "I never would have realized. You look so different. Your frame has changed and Jenna's hair was blond. That case was over almost as quickly as it started, so I don't have the details as solid in my mind. As soon as you were discovered and it seemed like your disappearance had been innocent, I stopped digging into that case."

Jenna nodded. "I understand. I wish I had known at the time that I wasn't being paranoid, that something really had been strange." She looked at Melissa. "It seemed strange that someone would offer to show me around and then we'd get lost, but female hikers don't worry about other female hikers."

Melissa smiled wickedly. "Exactly."

Cipher growled at her.

"I'd read you your rights, but I guess you already know them all," Sergeant Patrick said.

"I'll happily remind her," Jenna spoke up. "You're under arrest for the murder of Tori McDaniel, as well as several others. You have the right to remain silent." She grabbed Melissa by the arm and hauled her toward the exit.

Sergeant Patrick followed.

"Apologies for suspecting you." Agent Hawkins approached Finn with a handshake. "I spoke with the special agent in charge in Anchorage. Your transfer is set to go through. You've earned it, especially after being looked at with suspicion when you'd done nothing wrong."

"We were only trying to follow—" Agent Littleton spoke up.

"Protocol," Finn finished. Smiled. "I know. And don't apologize. I'm happy to have been a suspect if it meant we got to this point somehow. However it happened."

"The information you had to leave for, the meeting at the police department... Do you think...?" Jordyn trailed off, but Finn was already nodding, seeming to have realized already what she suspected.

"It was planted by Melissa, I would guess. As was the note implicating me in Nicole Collins's death."

Agent Hawkins confirmed that. "We called APD on the way here once the pieces started to fall into place after Officer Lee left. Turns out Melissa pulled some strings to throw us off the trail. She has a friend at the Anchorage PD who told her about a guy who killed someone there. The friend didn't do anything wrong, but Melissa used the information to try to spin it as though the Anchorage PD was asking us to consider that suspect in our investigation, when in fact they weren't."

"Can we prove everything?" Jordyn asked, not sure if she could really relax yet, if this was really over.

Agent Littleton had bent down beside Tori's body. "Bracelet around the ankle matches the description of the one the missing person was reported to have been wearing. If DNA matches…should go a long way to confirming things."

Finn didn't answer for a long moment. Jordyn realized his eyes were trained to Tori's remains. She watched a single tear trail its way down his cheek. She wished she could brush it away. But he needed to grieve. To say goodbye and let her go. They both did.

"We'll have work to do to build a case," Finn finally said to Jordyn. "But yes, we can prove it. She'll go to prison, and she won't ever get to leave."

It was small consolation, Jordyn realized as her eyes went to the bones again. Tori had lost her life. So had all those other women. Melissa was only losing her freedom. It wasn't enough. Beside the bones, Finn was sitting on the ground, staring. She could see the tears on his cheeks.

Jordyn kept staring at the bones too, glancing at Finn now and then. Finally, he stood, wiped his cheeks and looked over at her, shook his head. "Nothing will bring her back. But at least it's over now. No one else will have to go through this," Finn said to her softly, like he was reading her facial expressions. And maybe he was. He'd certainly proven enough times that he knew her better than he had any right to after the short time they'd spent together.

So why would he keep pushing her away?

"I know," she said. "I know she's not coming back. None of them are." They both went quiet. Jordyn felt a sense of calm come over her. She wouldn't say she felt entirely at peace. Life was still heartbreaking, and today's events would take some time to think through and unpack. Had it really been this morning she and Finn had gone to search and found the body of the most recent victim? That would have been an emotionally exhausting day all on its own, never mind all that had just happened with Melissa. Not to mention earlier…almost kissing him, searching some more, actually kissing him…

That kiss. It was another heartbreak on top of all the others she'd experienced today. She and Finn could have been a fantastic team. Maybe she'd have even been brave enough to see how it went, give their relationship a chance, but Agent Hawkins's words earlier about his transfer going through reminded her that could never be a possibility, not when her life was here in this town, and even if she were willing to give it up, it wasn't as though Finn had asked her to. He was going to leave when this was over, and he was going to leave alone. Jordyn's heart squeezed as she thought of him. So much of how they operated was similar, but enough was different that she thought they complemented each other well. They both knew where the other was coming from, knew their darkest days, because they'd had the same ones. Only at the time, they hadn't had each other to walk through them with.

That was the reason she was able to stand here and not fall entirely apart in the face of the evil she'd just looked in the eye, the evidence of how cruel humans could be. It was a combination of knowing that even if there was never going to be anything between them, Finn was going to be here as all of this was dealt with, and the realization Jordyn had had about God earlier today, that He was in control and she was not.

If He was in control, did that include romantic relationships too?

She stole a wistful glance at Finn. Found herself praying. *God, maybe we aren't supposed to be anything more than friends. Maybe we just needed to be here for each other these last few days, but if we were...if we are...help? Do something?*

"You'll have to give a statement, but for now, what do you say we get out of here?" Finn asked, as he reached down to pet Cipher, who'd been sitting patiently beside Jordyn, waiting for her next instruction.

Jordyn nodded, sadness warring with the relief that this was finally over.

That finally, maybe, she could figure out what it meant to move on.

The last few days were finally catching up to Finn, who was trying to keep his strides long enough to keep up with Cipher, who was trotting through the woods, vest off, job done, as they made their way to the trailhead.

"She's okay to walk a bit farther ahead," Jordyn said. "We don't have to run."

They were well away from the canyon now. Finn would probably go back to help process the scene. His parents might want to see Tori, or they might not. He didn't know how they'd react, but for him, the place hadn't been a place of nightmares at all. Tori had been gone for years. Not gone, he reminded himself again. She'd been in Heaven for years. But they'd all still been here, without closure, without peace.

Closure, they now had. But he was realizing that peace was going to have to come from God. Hopefully today, the conversation he'd had with the Lord earlier, would be the start of Finn realizing peace came from Him.

Which meant it wouldn't come from running away. Wouldn't come from leaving Alaska.

He glanced at Jordyn.

It was hardly romantic, talking about relationships with all they'd been through today. Besides, just because he wished he could go back to that kiss earlier today and not push Jordyn away, didn't mean that was what Jordyn wanted. Maybe she was happier leaving things as they were.

Cipher stayed in sight, but Finn slowed down.

"You okay?" Jordyn asked.

"Just tired. You?"

"Pretty tired too," she said.

And Finn didn't know if it was a hint—he'd never been great at reading women—all he knew was that he wanted another chance, and she was walking beside him, almost close enough that their arms were brushing.

Maybe…maybe he could take a chance. He wrapped his arm around her, letting his palm rest on her shoulder. "Better?"

Jordyn stopped walking and turned toward him. She stared up at him earnestly.

"What do you want, Finn? I don't understand." Her face was close. Only inches away. But he wouldn't kiss her, not now. If he did, he wouldn't say what he needed to say.

"You're right. I'm sorry. I'm sorry about earlier."

"If you're apologizing for that kiss again…" She'd looked away from him, but if he was reading the expression on her face right, and understanding her words right, it wasn't something she thought he should be sorry for.

"I'm not. I'm definitely not. I'm apologizing for the fact that I apologized for it in the first place."

"You're…what?"

Finn cleared his throat. "Nothing about the last week has been easy or ideal or something I'd want to repeat again—with one exception. I'm so glad it was your dog who found me in that clearing. And not just because I think Cipher is fantastic." He laughed a little. "But I'm glad because it brought you back into my life. You fascinated me the whole time we were growing up. I had the worst crush on you."

Jordyn smiled. "You're kidding. I had one on you."

Finn shrugged. "Guess we should have said something."

"Or maybe not," Jordyn said, looking up and meeting his eyes now. "I don't know about you, but I had a lot I needed to learn, things I needed to go through… Today changed things for me. I had to surrender to God, realize He's the one in control of my life and I'm not. Would I have done that if we'd been in each other's lives before now? I don't know. But it needed to happen, and I wouldn't change it."

She hadn't stepped away from his arm, which gave him an extra boost of confidence.

"So you weren't sorry about the kiss?" he said.

"Were you?" she asked. "Actually sorry?"

Without looking away, Finn slowly shook his head. "I wasn't sorry. In fact, I'd like to kiss you again. If that's okay."

"I want that too, but…" She hesitated, and he could read in her eyes that she was debating something.

"I'm not leaving," he said. "I'm going to meet with my boss as soon as I can and withdraw my transfer request for sure. Alaska is where I belong."

"Because you love the state?"

Finn reached down, took both of her hands in his. "Because you are here. And I want to be where you are. Because I think I'm falling in love with you."

This time, she kissed him. And he definitely wasn't sorry. Not at all.

"Not too late?" he asked her when they pulled away, smiling at her while she smiled back.

Jordyn shook her head and laughed, then closed the distance between them again for another kiss. "Too late? No. I would say you were right on time."

When they started walking again, it was hand in hand, and Finn knew there were still questions to be answered. Would he stay with the FBI? Maybe get a job at the Eagle Bend Police Department? He'd have to talk to Jordyn, see what she thought. The only thing he was sure of right now was that he was relieved this was over and they were safe. This investigation had pushed him back to the God he'd loved so much but had walked away from. It had also pushed him toward the woman he loved, and he wanted to spend the rest of his life, if she'd have him, adventuring around this state with Jordyn Williams.

The path that had led them here wasn't one he would have predicted. But God, Finn was realizing, had His own ways of allowing things to happen. God knew what He was doing.

And for that, Finn was thankful.

\* \* \* \* \*

*If you enjoyed*
Hunting a Killer
*be sure to check out other books
by Sarah Varland, including*
K-9 Alaskan Defense
*Available now from Love Inspired Suspense!*

Dear Reader,

Thank you for reading another book! I appreciate that we share a love of reading, especially Christian fiction, and can't thank you enough for picking up one of my books to read when you have so many choices out there. I really enjoyed Finn and Jordyn's story, because they seemed like such a fun couple to me. I used the word "partnership" a lot when Finn and Jordyn were wrestling with their feelings toward each other, and I thought it was interesting how these characters were such a good team. I loved writing a couple like that.

Something else I enjoyed writing in this book in particular was the faith thread. Both characters struggle with the idea of God being truly in control of their lives. Their struggles overlap somewhat, but they look different in each character's life. I think many of us share the same struggle. We like to put our faith in God theoretically but hold back from truly trusting in Him, even in the little things in life. I hope as you read the story, you were reminded (or told for the first time) that God is trustworthy. And that you are very much loved by God. If you don't know Him for yourself, I pray you would come to know Him.

I love hearing from you! More times than I can count an encouraging email has come in from a reader at just the right time when I need to hear it. Some of you have shared real stories from your life with me, like your visits to Alaska, and I love hearing about them. Thank you for sharing and feel free to email anytime at sarahvarland@gmail.com. You can also find me on Instagram, @sarahvarland, or on Facebook, @sarahvarlandauthor.

I hope you enjoyed the book!
*Sarah Varland*

# Get up to 4 Free Books!

### We'll send you 2 free books from each series you try PLUS a free Mystery Gift.

**FREE**
Value Over
**$25**

Both the **Love Inspired®** and **Love Inspired® Suspense** series feature compelling novels filled with inspirational romance, faith, forgiveness and hope.